FOOLPROOF

by

PHILIP DANIELS

St. Martin's Press
New York

Library of Congress Cataloging-in-Publication Data

Daniels, Philip.
Foolproof / Philip Daniels.
p.   cm.
"A Thomas Dunne book."
ISBN 0-312-13077-5
I. Title.
PR6054.A522F66   1995
823'.914—dc20   95-14715   CIP

First published in Great Britain by
Robert Hale Limited

First U.S. Edition: August 1995
10   9   8   7   6   5   4   3   2   1

FOOLPROOF

ONE

Charlie Hurst slowed the car as he reached the red-brick wall. There was a house-sign beside the open iron gates. Applefield. This was the place, all right. Turning the wheel carefully, he pointed the silver Mercedes into the drive and parked at the front of the house. He switched off the engine, and put the keys in his pocket with some relief. Not the world's best driver, he much preferred to sit in the back, and let Irish Tony, or even Mad Jimmy Evans do the work. But this geezer had said he was to come alone. So here he was. And very nice, too.

He closed the door carefully, enjoying the luxury of leaving it unlocked. This was a long way from Clapham. Not too many car thieves in this neck of the woods. People in houses like this didn't have to go in for that kind of thieving. These were the big dealers. Property, stock exchange, stuff like that. They didn't even call it thieving. They called it business.

As he mounted the stone steps to the small terrace, a large strange-looking bird stalked disdainfully away. He'd seen a bird like that somewhere before, all those coloured feathers sticking out of its backside. Peacock, that's what it was. A bleeding peacock. This bloke must be loaded.

"You're Charlie Hurst, aren't you?"

Turning, he saw a tall man about his own age looking at him.

"Yup," he agreed. "Was that a peacock?"

"Probably," grinned the other, "there are several around somewhere. I'm Jeremy Newton, by the way. Do come in."

Charlie followed his host into the spacious hallway and through a door leading off at the side. Newton closed the door behind him.

"Please sit down," he invited. "Can I get you a drink? Scotch all right?"

The visitor sank into a heavy red leather chair. To his surprise, it was very comfortable.

"Not Scotch, if you don't mind. Not in the afternoon. Glass of beer would be nice."

"Good idea. I'll join you. Have any trouble finding the place?"

The two men were measuring each other up as they spoke. Charlie Hurst was an inch shorter than Newton, with hair as black as the other's was fair. The square chunky face conveyed rugged honesty, and this had always been an extra card in his hand. Rugged he certainly was, but honesty was not a strong feature of his nature. Newton longer in the face, with a hooked nose and a good chin.

"Trouble? No. Once I left the motorway, I just followed your directions. Very clear. Oh, ta."

Charlie took the glass. Some kind of lager by the look of it. Ah well, didn't matter. Hadn't come here to drink, anyway.

"Well, cheers."

"Cheers."

They each took a sip, and Newton seated himself opposite the visitor, folding one fawn-clad leg negligently over the other.

"Good of you to come," he began.

"Not much choice really. You made it sound like one of those offers you can't refuse, know what I mean? What's it all about, anyway?"

Newton offered cigarettes, and they both lit up.

"First of all, let me explain that I've been looking for you for two years."

Two years. Charlie's mind began to race. What had he been doing two years ago? Was this some kind of revenge this bloke was up to?

"Don't look so alarmed, Charlie—you don't mind if I call you Charlie?"

"Help yourself, Jeremy."

He wasn't going to be talked down to.

"Fine. I ought to tell you that I'm a very ambitious man. I've spent a great deal of time working out a plan to realise these ambitions. But I can't do it alone. I need a man with, shall we say, special qualifications. It took me a long time to find him. And now you're here."

Hurst relaxed—a little. What did he mean, special qualifications?

"Go on, then. What's your proposition?"

Newton tapped ash delicately into a floor-standing

receptacle.

"We have a lot in common, Charlie. We're the same age for a start, as near as damn it. I was thirty-three last month, you'll be the same in six weeks' time."

If the listener was impressed, his face betrayed nothing.

"And?"

"We've both come a long way, by different routes. I'm reasonably well known in my professional circles. You're well known in other places. I made my way with pieces of paper—examinations. You made yours with your fists, and your native intelligence. Very different methods, most people would agree. But there are plenty of men as well qualified as me, and they're not living in my style. There are equally as many with your guts, and yet they don't occupy your position in. the world. So you and I have something extra, what the advertising people would call the mysterious added ingredient."

Charlie grinned faintly.

"Oh yes? What might that be, then?"

Newton looked him squarely in the eye.

"We're a pair of ruthless bastards. We don't let anything stand in our way. We get rid of the opposition. Squash it."

He was taking a chance, talking like that, reflected Charlie. There weren't many people around who would call him a ruthless bastard. Not to his face. But somehow, he wasn't offended. This Jeremy was beginning to interest him. Might be something in all this.

"You said you know a lot about me. What, for instance?"

Newton grinned.

"I could go on for half an hour," he claimed, "but it shouldn't be necessary. Let's say, for one thing, I know about number three, Parkside South."

"How did you—"

"Never mind, I know. That should be sufficient."

Charlie swallowed. The address was one where a certain Mr. Patrick Owen stayed when he was up from the country on business. He used the place as a casual overnight stop. It was particularly useful if there was a special lady who had to be careful of her movements, because of husbands and other complications. Mr. Patrick Owen kept himself to himself, and no one in London was supposed to know him, except Charlie Hurst, because Mr. Owen and Charlie were one and the same man.

"Any more little tricks like that?" he queried.

There was one thing Mr. Clever-Sod Newton didn't know. Couldn't know, Charlie was sure of that.

Newton smiled.

"How about the deal you made with King-size Saunders?"

Charlie let out a long breath, and stared at him, speechless for the moment. The rivalry betweeen Saunders and himself was public knowledge. People watched, and wondered, and kept their distance. It was obvious to everybody that things could only end in bloody riot. The unanswered question was, which of the two would be left standing when the dust died

down? Or would they both be finished? The odds on
that were probably even, and they both knew it. That
was why they'd made their agreement, so that they
could sleep without gun or knife under the pillow. But
nobody must know, it was a personal secret.

"Jeremy son, your mouth is going to get you in
trouble, one of these days."

Charlie Hurst spoke very quietly, but the words fell
off his tongue like poisoned darts. Newton's face
remained impassive.

"Keeping my own counsel is a large part of my job.
You never need to worry about me. It was really
your—um—arrangement with Mr. Saunders that
decided me finally to ask you here today."

"Go on talking," said Hurst. He did not relax his
tense pose.

Newton ground out his cigarette.

"You are maturing, Charlie. You've come a long
way, and it's been hard. Painful, too, a lot of it. But
you've always made it more painful for other people
than for yourself. You're an important man, now. No
need to rush about quite so much. No call for so much
of the old violence. Plenty coming in every week, far
more than me, so why not sit back a little? Enjoy life for
a change. That's the way you've been thinking, isn't
it?"

"What if I have? What's wrong with that?"

Charlie's tone was truculent. His host made a
deprecatory gesture.

"Nothing. It's as I said. A sign of maturity. But it
wouldn't have happened three years ago. Even two

years ago. You'd have gone after King-size then, and somebody would have been going to a funeral."

It was true, and Hurst knew it.

"What're you trying to say? That I'm afraid of Saunders? Because, if you are—"

"Not a bit of it. What I'm saying is, you're starting to use the old grey matter. There's a time to fight, and a time to talk. You've done your share of fighting. Why shouldn't you enjoy the proceeds?"

Well, that was all right then. Long as this geezer didn't think he was going soft. In Charlie's world, any suggestion of that kind was an open invitation to every hard case in the parish.

"Let's suppose—only suppose, mind—that you're right. Why should I be interested in this job of yours?"

"Because, my friend, my proposition guarantees you security for life. For as long as you live, Charlie. And no fear of the law."

Talk. Charlie had heard that one before. Just this one job, lads, and we'll all live in clover for ever. All we have to do is tunnel into the Bank of England, or slip the Crown Jewels in our pockets one wet afternoon. The Big Job, in capital letters, was a strong part of the folklore in Charlie's world. A myth. It always had been, and it always would be. Look at the Great Train Robbery.

"Oh yes?" he replied, with heavy sarcasm. "Gonna sell Buckingham Palace, are we? I find the Arabs, and you draw up the papers, that it?"

"Not quite," grinned Newton. "It's an attractive

idea, but perhaps we ought to put it to one side for future reference. Before I go into details, let me tell you a little about myself.''

About time, too. This had all been one-sided up to now.

"I'm listening."

"Look around," invited Jeremy. "What do you think this place is worth?"

The visitor had made a mental assessment the moment he laid eyes on the place.

"Hundred grand?" he hazarded.

"Bit more, actually. But don't get the wrong idea, like many people do. That doesn't mean I've got a hundred thousand. It means that's what I'm worth, dead. Not much use to me then, is it?"

Charlie could see an immediate argument.

"You could flog it," he suggested. "Put the money in your pocket."

"And then what? I have to live somewhere, and it has to be somewhere I can invite people. So I buy another house, and I'm back where I started."

"What about a smaller place?"

Jeremy shook his head.

"It won't do. People in a certain way of life are expected to live up to it. My family expect it too. Wife, the children, everybody. No, I can look like a hundred thousand, live like a hundred thousand, but every penny I earn is spoken for. In case you find that hard to believe, look at your own sister's position."

The sudden reference to Eileen caught Hurst off balance.

"What's she got to do with it?"

"Nice house in Bromley. What's it worth, forty thousand, forty-five?"

"'Bout that," agreed Charlie, grudgingly.

"But she and her husband haven't got that kind of money, have they? Couldn't even afford to go on holiday last year."

That was true, reflected Charlie. There was some truth in what this Jeremy was saying. The side revelation that he knew about Eileen was accepted without question. A man who knew about him and King-size Saunders was likely to know anything.

"So according to you then, you're boracic. Broke, that is."

"Not broke, no. Committed. Nothing to spare. I don't like that. Things won't change much either. In ten years I'll be a full partner. There'll be a bit more money then, but I don't want to wait. I want it now. I want a lot of money, not just a few more thousand a year."

Now they were starting to talk about money, and the man from Clapham felt on more familiar ground.

"How much money?"

"A million pounds."

Nice round sum. Charlie pursed his lips.

"And what's my end?"

"The same. One million for me, one million for you."

He might have known it. This was going to be a take-on. One of these Crown Jewels dreams. Pity. It had been shaping up, until now. Quite promising.

"Who do we have to kill?" he asked.

"Nobody. There'll be no violence. Practically no risk, either."

The word 'practically' rang like a counterfeit coin among the other words.

"No risk for you, you mean. I'm the one who takes the chances, that it?"

"Small chances, believe me. I'll explain about that, in its turn. Do you know much about the stock market, Charlie?"

He would sooner have had more details about those little risks. Still, he'd have to wait, by the sound of it.

"Stock market?" he echoed. "Not much. Big gambling take-on for blokes with posh voices, innit? Most of the punters come unstuck, a few of the big boys make a bomb. Every now and then one of 'em gets spotted, and does twelve months. Only when he comes out, he's got fifty million quid in his sky."

"Sky?"

"Sky rocket. Pocket," explained the speaker, grinning. "Anyway, that's what it all looks like to me."

Jeremy Newton considered this definition. It wasn't the most informed view he'd ever heard, but it suited his purpose very well to have his future partner thinking that way.

"That isn't bad at all," he conceded. "Rather a black view of things, but realistic. It's a very treacherous area for people who don't know what they're doing. Like horse-racing. Come to think of it, horse-racing is very similar in many ways. And I know you're an expert on that."

Charlie nodded.

"Expert enough to know it's a mug's game. Fifty quid now and then, just for a giggle, but you'd never catch me putting any real money on."

The man opposite pointed.

"But let's take an unusual case. Supposing there's a certain horse which you know is going to win. That would change things, wouldn't it?"

Ah, thought Charlie, that's a punter talking. Mister average mug who thinks knowing the winner in advance will make him a fortune. Glad of the opportunity to take up the rôle of lecturer, instead of listener, he shook his head sadly.

"They all think that. Sell the house, sell the car, sell the missus—if you can find any takers—and put the lot on his nose. Make your fortune overnight. Silly people."

Jeremy looked sceptical.

"You wouldn't do that?"

"No way," was the positive reply. "Think about it. Suddenly, out of nowhere, some geezer nobody ever heard of puts down ten grand, twenty grand on a gee-gee. It wins. He's due a lot of money. Those bookies are not mugs, you know. They think to themselves, Hallo, here's young Basil, never put more than a pound on in his life, suddenly we owe him fifty grand, a hundred grand, whatever it is. They wonder about young Basil. Perhaps he knew something they didn't know. So they get naughty."

"They refuse to pay, you mean?"

"Depends on who we're talking about. The big firms, they'll have a chat with the bogies, ask 'em to have a sniff round. They get on to the stewards, the Jockey Club, race-course narks, all the hounds. Young Basil gets a lot of visitors. So does the trainer, the owner, the jockey. There's hell to pay all round."

The other considered this, frowning.

"You said the big firms," he reminded. "What about the others?"

"Ah well." Charlie gave a shrug. "Some of them might not waste a lot of money on telephone calls. They might make a few enquiries of their own. Take my word, young Basil's better off with the coppers than he's going to be with some of them blokes."

Jeremy was evidently impressed.

"So you don't think it would be worth knowing?"

"Never said that," denied the speaker. "Meself, I'd have five hundred on him, couple of hundred on something else, make it look good. When I win, they'll say, 'He's a fly bugger, that Charlie. Made a nice score today.' But they won't think naughties."

"Ah."

There was silence for a few moments. Charlie Hurst thought his host was turning over this information, adjusting to some new ideas. He was not to know that what he had been doing was to spell out, in almost identical terms, the proposition that Jeremy was about to lay before him. Except that the subject would not be horse-racing.

Before Jeremy could speak, the door behind them opened.

Charlie had read a story once where a woman's voice had been described as silk being rubbed against velvet. The image had always stuck in his mind.

A voice said, "I'm sorry, darling. I didn't realise you had a visitor."

Charlie turned his head, and had his first lingering view of Mara Newton.

TWO

She stood in the doorway, appraising him with her eyes. So this was Jeremy's tough guy, the one he wouldn't let her meet. From the way he'd been described, she'd half-expected some hulking bruiser with a broken nose and cauliflower ears. This one wasn't like that at all. Almost as tall as Jeremy, thirty-five or so, with the wildest black hair above a craggy, challenging face. The eyes, which were drinking her in, were deep blue and filled with—what—challenge? The light grey suit had cost him a fortune. Pity about the shirt, and the tie was, of course, a disaster. But still—

Jeremy tried to conceal his annoyance. Mara knew damned well he didn't want her in there. Aloud, he said, "Sorry, love, I forgot to mention it. Come and say hallo to Patrick Owen."

Mara had given some thought to her appearance. Since she wasn't supposed to be expecting a visitor, she couldn't very well tart herself up too much. There was a pair of faded dungarees which had shrunk in the last wash. She could no longer work in them, because they

were too tight everywhere, but she could wear them for
a brief appearance, and to the considerable advantage
of her lithe and compact figure. An open-necked shirt
revealed not too much of the brown throat, and her feet
were bare.

"How do you do, Mr. Owen."

'Mr. Owen' took the slim brown hand briefly, and
smiled. Nice teeth.

"How do you do, Mrs. Newton."

And he hadn't said 'pleased to meet you' either.
Better all the time.

Her husband watched the performance with
impatience. Blast the woman. He'd told her quite
clearly to keep out of the way.

"I don't suppose it occurred to Jeremy to offer you
any tea," Mara said brightly. "May I get you some?"

'Mr. Owen' kept a tight grip on himself. Birds had
always been a source of great trouble to him, and this
was no ordinary bird. But he hadn't come here to drink
tea. He looked over at Jeremy, uncertain.

"No thanks, dear," was the firm decision from that
quarter. "We thought we'd have a cold beer instead."

And I'm not going to offer you one, either, thought
Jeremy savagely. Go away. He flashed her a warning
glance.

Mara smiled, making for the door.

"Oh well then, if you're sure. I'm sorry I disturbed
you. Perhaps we'll meet again, Mr. Owen."

"I hope so, Mrs. Newton."

Beautiful, thought Charlie.

Bitch, thought Jeremy. Well, at least she'd taken the

hint.

"Sorry about that," he said, as the door closed.

"Sorry about what?" queried Charlie. "I'm glad I didn't miss seeing your wife. Trip wasn't wasted, even if we don't do business."

Jeremy was uncertain how to take that, so he smiled vaguely, and put Mara out of his mind. The mention of business brought them back to the matter in hand.

"Well then, let's talk, and we'll soon know. I liked your little exposé about the gambling scene, when it comes to horse-racing. It will help us with our own scheme, I'm sure."

Charlie was not nearly so sure. He didn't even know what the scheme was.

"I'll be a better judge of that when I know what we're talking about."

The timing was right, decided Newton.

"We're talking about gambling. Stock Exchange gambling, except that we shall know who's going to win."

The man from Clapham made a face.

"What's my end? Do I inject dope into the stock-brokers?"

"Nothing so crude," replied Jeremy, unsmiling. "You provide information. I will tell you where and when to find it. You pass it to me, I act on it, and we're home."

There was an objection there, straight away.

"If you're going to tell me where this stuff is, why do you need me at all? Why don't you just go and get it yourself?"

It was a fair question, and Jeremy said as much.

"Fair point, and I'll come to it. First, the background. The Stock Exchange works on share prices, for the purpose of our chat today. A share might be worth, say fifty pence one morning. By the close of business that afternoon it has become worth sixty pence. All kinds of things influence a change like that, and most of them don't concern me. But you can see what it means?"

Charlie shrugged.

"Sure. Somebody makes ten pee. Big deal."

His lecturer was uncertain whether the point had really been missed, or whether his prospective partner was being facetious.

"If he has one share, yes. If he has a hundred thousand shares, as we would have, he makes ten thousand pounds."

That brought him a low whistle.

"And the net outlay," Jeremy continued, "is the cost of two telephone calls. One in the morning, with instructions to buy. One in the afternoon, to sell."

"Sounds all right when you say it quick," objected the other. "But you have to cough up the cash in the first place."

His host smiled.

"Not so," he corrected gently. "The only commitment is a promise to pay. And it doesn't have to be kept, because at the end of the transaction you make a profit. They have to pay you."

There were fifty more questions Charlie would have liked to ask, but he realised he was going to have to take

Newton's word for much of that end of things. After all, he reasoned, Newton would be the one making the phone calls, he'd be the one sticking his neck out so far as paying up was concerned. Let him worry about the details.

"All right then, if you say so. Let's get back to this share. How do we know it'll go up?"

Jeremy was relieved not to have the task of explaining the intricacies of the dealing process. None of that was any of this chap's concern, and obviously he was quick-witted enough to realise it.

"As I said earlier, all kinds of factors can come into the picture. Knowing in advance for instance what a company report is going to say, that can be very valuable. Knowing that a certain key-man has decided to retire or to go and work for some rival firm. Money in the bank, that kind of information."

Information. Charlie's ears pricked up. This was where he came in.

"And that's my end," he contributed. "You tell me which geezer will know what's going on, I put the frighteners on him, tell you, and we clean up."

The horror on Newton's face was unforced.

"God no," he protested. "Nothing like that. Nothing obvious, and certainly no violence. A simple burglary will tell us all we need to know."

"Burglary?"

"Yes. All we need is access to documents. Minutes of meetings, memos, summaries of accounts, that kind of thing."

"You want me to nick 'em? But even if I do, and I

don't say I will, they'll know something's up. Be like the bookies all over again. They watch the betting the next day, whoever makes a score gets his collar felt. Tell me if I'm wrong."

He leaned back, satisfied that he had made a valid point. In a way, he was right.

But he was unprepared for Jeremy's beam of approval.

"Exactly," he enthused. "Couldn't have summed it up better myself."

"Well then—" mumbled Charlie in a puzzled tone.

"But it won't be exactly like that," explained the smiling Newton. "The papers will not be stolen. They will merely be disturbed by a burglar in the normal search for valuables. Let me show you something."

He got up from his chair and went to a mahogany bureau in one corner of the room. Opening a drawer, he lifted something out, closed the drawer and came back to the watching man.

He held out his hand for inspection. Charlie stared at the small black oblong.

"Know what this is?"

"Looks like a toy camera. Kid's thing."

"Yes, it does, I agree. And you're right about it's being a camera. But it's anything but a toy. It's the very latest, most efficient miniature camera in the world today. German, naturally. This gadget can take fifty pictures of the highest possible definition. It cost me eleven hundred pounds. But, for you—" and he dropped his voice neatly into the whine of a street pedlar—"for you, a special price."

Charlie grinned, taking the tiny box and examining it.

"Oh yes," he scoffed. "Tell me about this big favour."

"To you, it's free," Jeremy explained, in his normal tone. "It goes with the job. I want you to photograph everything you find. At first, that is. After a while, you'll come to know what matters and what doesn't."

The man in the chair put the camera back in his hand.

"Wish you'd sit down," he grumbled, "I don't like people standing over me."

"Certainly."

When they were facing each other on the same level again, Charlie pointed a finger.

"Let's get this straight. First of all, I do a bit of breaking and entering. Then I photograph all the papers I can find. After that I nick a few bits and pieces to make it look real. Yes?"

"That is the intention," confirmed Newton.

"But what's all this about me getting the hang of it after a while. You mean there's more than one job?"

"Oh yes. Most definitely."

The confirmation did not please the listener.

"Well, before I give you an argument, tell me why," he invited.

Newton leaned forward, as if to give emphasis to what he was going to say.

"Because of your own point, the one you made earlier. We couldn't come on strong on just one deal. People would know there was something fishy going on. We have to show nice profits, the kind of profits that can be expected from people taking a reasonable gamble. People with good market knowledge, who are prepared to back up their judgement with hard cash. But it mustn't be big enough to make others suspicious. Not even to make them wonder."

Charlie gave himself a few moments to think about this.

"I don't know," he said finally. "Never been a burglar, not my line. I could get nicked. Then what?"

His companion nodded soberly.

"Yes, you could. I shall try to make it as foolproof as possible. The chance of your being caught will be very slim. But if you are, what will happen? You have no prison record. The police know all about you, naturally, they're not fools. But you have no record, whatever they might think. And they will be as surprised as everybody else to find Charlie Hurst up on a simple burglary charge. You might get six months, and you'll serve four. I'm prepared to compensate you when you come out."

"How much?"

"If you get caught on your first outing, five thousand pounds out of my own pocket. After that, it shouldn't be necessary. You'll have your own share of whatever we've earned to come out to."

"And you don't know how much that'll be?"

"No. I only know it'll be well worth having."

It all seemed wrong, somehow. Sitting there, in that posh room, with the deep carpets and the rich polished wood. Afternoon sun streaming through from the

garden. This sort of conversation ought to be held in
the far corner of a pub bar, or better still in the back
seat of somebody's motor-car. But despite his mis-
givings, Charlie Hurst was in no doubt as to the deadly
earnestness of the man facing him. Funny. If you saw
him walking down some street in the City, you'd put
him down as some typical straight git. Half of bitter,
and the golf-clubs in the car-boot. But it was in the
eyes. Charlie was a great believer in eyes when he was
dealing with people. And this man's eyes told him a lot.

Newton too was thinking. He had not been exagger-
ating when he said he'd been to a lot of trouble tracking
down the right man for this scheme. He had to be a
man who was brave and resourceful, and there were
many people who fell into that category. But this man
needed to have more, needed to have a measure of
intelligence far above the norm, and that had made the
hunting much more difficult. On top of all that, the
candidate had to be a man who could carry off his new
wealth, once he had it. A man who could grow into his
money, as it were. Jeremy Newton wanted to be able to
relax for the rest of his life. He didn't want to be looking
over his shoulder, waiting for his erstwhile partner to
arrive and start blackmailing him, simply because he'd
managed to squander his own loot.

"I've still not heard why you're talking to me,"
Charlie reminded him. "Plenty of burglars about."

"That's true," conceded Jeremy, "but the only ones
I would know about would be the ones who get caught.
People the police can call on at any time, just on the
off-chance of a little stolen property. They'll never

think of you. It's not your style, and they know it.
That's the beauty of it, Charlie. Nobody will think of
you, including your own circles. Can you imagine it,
Charlie Hurst turning burglar for a couple of hundred
pounds' worth of loot? Beneath your dignity, Charlie.
Everybody knows it. You'd bet that much on a good
brag hand, if you felt like it."

It was just the right mixture of truth and flattery to
register with the listening man, and Jeremy had
thought it out well beforehand.

"You're right there," agreed Charlie thoughtfully.
"I'd be a mug to stick my neck out for that sort of
dough, wouldn't I?"

"Exactly. You'll be the last man in London anybody
will think of."

Hurst nodded. It was true what this geezer was
saying. He would have to give this a very serious look.
He'd been around plenty of people over the years who
were always talking about the Big One. Some of the
plans he'd heard would make your hair stand on end.
Now and then, not often, but now and then, somebody
would come up with a winner. A good sound plan with
every chance of coming off. And then what happened?
Sometimes they got nobbled at the start because some
punter was late for work, or something stupid like that.
Other times, it all went like clockwork. The laddoes got
away with the loot, and everything would look smooth.
But one man would let them all down. It never failed.
Somebody got himself drunk, and talked. Somebody
started flashing his money about, or took off with some
floozie, leaving his missus in the cart. Somebody

always did something. And when they did, the law was waiting. That was all they needed, just the one little mistake, then they moved in, like a pack of starving wolves. Charlie had lost count of the number of jobs which had been scuppered, not because the idea was bad, or the information was wrong, but because of people. That was one reason he was coming round to liking the sound of this new venture. No people. Just himself, and this Jeremy Newton. He knew he would be all right, personally. Newton was a stranger, but look what he stood to lose. He was taking a real gamble. What he would be doing would be to put up his whole career, his reputation, the lot. So he must have a great opinion of their chances.

"I'll tell you what, Jeremy, you're beginning to interest me. I'm not saying yes, mind, but then again I'm not saying no. Have to think about it. No rush, is there?"

Newton was pleased with this reaction, because it gave him the opportunity to make one final, telling point. He shook his head.

"None," he affirmed. "That's the beauty of the whole proposition. There is no timing involved. We could start next week. Or we could leave it a month, a year for that matter. The framework doesn't alter."

Better and better, Charlie decided. He always liked time to think.

"How will I get in touch? Can I phone you here?"

"Absolutely not." The rejection was immediate. "My wife is a splendid woman in many ways, but she mustn't get wind of this. Nobody must. This is something for you and me. No third parties, and most particularly no women. If we pull this, we're going to be rich men, and it won't have to be a secret. We can show anyone, including the Fraud Squad, exactly where every penny came from, and it will all be absolutely legitimate. The only people who will ever know that anything was wrong will be us. You and me, Charlie."

In other words, no people. And that suited Charlie down to the ground.

"That makes sense. Where do I call you then?"

"At the office. If I'm not there, just leave a message for me to call Mr. Owen. I will call you at the flat between six and eight that same evening."

"All right." Charlie rose to go, looking around as he did so. "Always fancied myself in a place like this."

"You can do better than this. The sky's the limit, if we both stick to the rules. Just one more thing before you go."

Hallo. Charlie's instincts became alert again. This was going to be the fly in the ointment.

"What's that, then?"

Jeremy smiled good-naturedly.

"Don't be so suspicious. I thought you might be interested in picking up a little cash. Absolutely no risk whatever. All you have to do is walk in and take it. I can tell you all the details, and I don't want a share. Call it my way of showing how deadly serious I am about all this. A sign of good faith if you like."

Charlie relaxed, but only a little.

"No harm in listening," he shrugged.

It was another ten minutes before he left the house. The car looked well, standing out in front with the afternoon sun reflecting from it. Yes, he decided, it all went well together. The car, and the house, and him. Charlie Hurst. Property owner, that would be a giggle. He looked quickly around for signs of that luscious bird Newton was married to. Wouldn't mind owning a bit of that property, he decided. Ah well. Plenty more like her, when a man had a few quid in his pocket. He opened the car door.

From an upstairs window Mara Newton watched thoughtfully.

THREE

Old Mr. Pettiford examined his pocket-watch and checked it carefully against the heavy wooden wall-clock over the office door.

"Twelve o'clock," he announced.

It was a daily ritual which he had observed for more years than he could accurately remember. Nobody knew exactly how long Mr. Pettiford had been in these rooms, not even the senior partners, because he outdated everyone, but the time of the Crimean War was the most popularly subscribed belief. Legend had it that there had actually been a senior clerk before Mr. Pettiford's time, and that worthy had certainly assisted with the first draft of Magna Carta. There was an aura of timeless continuity about. Mr. Pettiford, from the rusty black of his jacket to the thinning white of his hair.

At midday he would proclaim the fact for the benefit of the people under his charge. It was the signal for the lunch-time parole of most of them. They would steam out from the buildings, leaving only the two private secretaries and Mr. Pettiford himself. At one o'clock—

'sharp, mind'—they would return, whereupon Mr. Pettiford, the private secretaries and the partners themselves would adjourn. The notable exception to this rule was Thursday, when the solemn ritual of the wages was performed. On that day, having collected the money, Mr. Pettiford would remain in his office, preparing the wage-packets in accordance with a list supplied by the cashier. Lunch would consist of one glass of very dry sherry and a small packet of thin sandwiches specially prepared in a nearby café.

On this particular Thursday, there was to be another departure from the routine. Instead of the disciplined scramble for the door, following his announcement, there was silence while one of the clerks addressed him.

"Excuse me, Mr. Pettiford, but you do remember that today is Mr. Cooper's party?"

Of course he remembered, thought Pettiford, irritably. Did this fool think he was in his dotage, or something? He remembered very well, but he still did not approve of these goings-on in the lunch-hour. Beyond the lunch-hour, dammit.

"Well, what of it?"

The other stood his ground.

"Mr. Cooper invited us all to meet him for a celebration drink at the Cloisters at one o'clock, sir. It means we shall all be late back."

"I am aware of the arrangement, thank you. However, I do not expect anyone to take undue advantage of the firm's generosity. Everyone is to be back behind their desk at one-thirty. Sharp, mind."

"I'll make sure that everyone is clear about that. Shall you be joining us, sir?"

No, he would not be joining them. There was nothing more calculated to stir up his dyspepsia than the sight and sound of a crowd of grinning, sweaty clerks in a public house. Not to mention the young women. It was not right for women to be permitted inside taverns at all, and he, Pettiford, was not going to lend sanction to such activities by his presence.

"It is wages day, as I'm sure you are aware. I shall convey my respects to Mr. Cooper in my own way. One-thirty sharp, now."

The rooms began to empty, and soon there was only the subdued clack-clack of distant typewriters to disturb him. Mr. Pettiford checked the cashier's list again, laboriously adding up the totals against each name, and without regard to the fact that the figures were already machine-checked. He had no time for machines, with their nasty square figures and odd ways of setting things out. You couldn't trust 'em.

"Can't think why you bother with all that," one of the senior partners had said to him once. "Machines can't make mistakes, you know."

"Quite true, sir. But they cannot make corrections, either. They can only process the information which is fed to them. That information is given by people, and people do make mistakes."

He had been successful, too, on one occasion. It must have been ten, no, twelve years ago. One junior clerk had been listed to receive one hundred pounds instead of ten. Mr. Pettiford had pounced on the error in a rare moment of pure joy. For him, the one discovery was more than justification for the hours of laborious checking.

There was no such error today. Eighteen hundred and thirty-one pounds, fifty-seven pence. He made his last meticulous tick at the foot of the column, and checked his watch again. Twelve-thirty. The bank was only fifty yards away, and his appointed time was twelve-twenty. Better be off. Unlocking the safe, he removed the anti-thief bag, and locked it to his wrist. It was a fearsome device, and the demonstration had quite startled him.

"Now, supposing you're walking along and somebody tries to snatch the bag. This is what happens."

There was a loud bang, and a spray of green liquid shot out of various hidden compartments. At the same instant, steel poles sprang out on telescopic legs, making the bag look like some grotesque piece of space hardware.

"A man would look a bit conspicuous, trying to carry that lot, and with green dye all over his face."

Mr. Pettiford thought privately it was a great deal of fuss to make over a simple journey of fifty yards, but the bag had been produced for his use, and he dutifully used it. A few moments later he was out in the lunch-time crowd, an inconspicuous figure.

In the window of the sandwich bar on the opposite side of the street, a man watched him emerge. Anyone would know the watcher for a tourist. He wore a panama hat, large dark glasses above a thick black moustache, and a hold-all slung over one shoulder.

Even Charlie Hurst's close acquaintances could have been forgiven for passing him by. He had never laid eyes on Mr. Pettiford before, but he had Jeremy Newton's description, and recalled his words very clearly.

"Just watch the doorway. He will come out between twenty and twenty-five past twelve, rely on it. Only something like World War Three could stop him."

Twelve twenty-two, and there he was. The bag was the clincher. Charlie stirred absently at the liquid sold to him as coffee, and waited. Ten minutes later, his inspection of a girl in a yellow dress almost caused him to miss the returning man. He was just in time to spot a rear view as Mr. Pettiford disappeared into the doorway. Everything according to the schedule. So far, so good. Charlie had nothing to do now for forty minutes. It would not be safe to enter the office too soon after one o'clock in case one of the second shift lunch-brigade was late leaving. Might as well go for a walk.

Safely back in the office, Mr. Pettiford unlocked the bag, and set the money out on his desk in readiness. He was soon absorbed in his counting and checking, and the minutes ticked away.

At ten past one an American tourist paused outside the buildings, reading the legend on the brass plate screwed into the wall. No one paid him any attention. London was packed with tourists checking up on its history. The tourist walked up the steps, and went inside. This was the crucial time, this was when it could go wrong. If anyone was working late, or returned early, he might be challenged. But there would be no panic, he'd simply have to abandon the project for some other Thursday. He was ostensibly looking for the room where the infamous Hanging Judge Jeffreys had once sat, if anyone should ask. He was in the wrong building, naturally, but would quickly be redirected, and off he would go with a grateful smile.

As it turned out, the cover story was not necessary. No one in the firm intended to miss Mr. Cooper's celebration. In the first place, he was a well-liked partner, and in the second place it was a rare and welcome break from the normal routine. At one-fourteen Charlie Hurst opened the door of the outer office and looked in. Empty. At the far end of the room, and glass-partitioned to ceiling height, was Mr. Pettiford's private office, the door firmly closed.

Charlie approached soundlessly, and could finally make out the figure of a seated man through the frosted glass. He hoped the old fool wasn't going to try being a hero. Grasping the door-handle, he stepped inside. Mr. Pettiford froze where he sat, with a half-filled glass of sherry in his hand.

"Afternoon, pop. Don't bother to get up."

The old man was not alarmed, merely annoyed at the interruption.

"Who are you, please, and what do you want? This is the lunch-period, you know."

"Sure, pop, I know. More private. Just carry on with your boozing, I won't tell anybody."

He placed the large hold-all on the desk.

"Look here—"

Irritated now, Mr. Pettiford began to rise from his chair.

"Sit down, old man. Look at this."

Charlie produced a heavy black revolver from the bag, and pointed it.

Mr. Pettiford subsided into his chair.

"Is this a hold-up?"

"You got it, dad. Just behave yourself, and nobody's going to get hurt. Not worth it, is it, just for a few hundred?"

Charlie began to scoop up the small brown envelopes and drop them into the hold-all. Mr. Pettiford's mind was racing. If he could delay this man somehow, perhaps some of the first-lunchers would come back early. If only he wasn't sitting down. There was an alarm bell behind the safe which ought to bring help. What about the fire alarm? Perhaps if he could get the fire alarm started—

"That's it, old-timer. Up on your feet."

The revolver was very steady in the thief's hand. Mr. Pettiford began to be afraid, for the first time.

"Are you going to—to—"

"No. I don't want to hurt you, pop. You've been real friendly. Just want you out of the way for a while. What's in there?"

Charlie pointed to a door in the corner.

"Why, nothing," protested the old man. "Really, nothing. It's only the stationery cupboard."

"That ought to do just swell. Get in there."

Mr. Pettiford didn't want to obey at all. Once in there he had no prospect of being able to baulk the villain. And the wages. Whatever would Mr. Banks say? He'd be disgraced of course, get the sack probably. The horror of such a possibility overcame his judgement.

"No," he cried, and launched himself at the revolver.

He had no chance. Charlie merely side-stepped, and swept the old man away from him as he sailed forward. Mr. Pettiford landed in a heap on the floor, a bent, pathetic figure, but Charlie had no time to waste on sympathy.

"Stupid old git," he breathed. "Now get in that cupboard, before I crack you over the head."

The senior clerk half shuffled, half crawled through the doorway. The intruder slammed it viciously behind him, feeling for the key. Damn. There wasn't one. Pushing the revolver into a side-pocket, he put his weight behind a steel filing-cabinet, inching it across the carpet until it blocked the door. Then he made a final check to ensure he'd left none of the money behind, swept up the hold-all and walked out. The whole thing had taken less than five minutes, so he ought not to meet anyone outside. All the same, it wouldn't do to be in a hurry. Despite his agitation, he forced himself to stroll quietly along the corridor leading to the street door, giving a sigh of relief as he opened it.

People were still hurrying by in both directions, intent upon a thousand urgent destinations. Charlie walked easily down the steps and joined them. For the first few yards he kept turning his head to inspect the doorway, half-expecting a horde of fist-waving citizens to emerge. But nothing happened, and soon he was just part of the human bloodstream of the city, just another dot in a swirling mass.

He walked as far as Charing Cross Station, threading his way among the taxis outside, and then up into the main concourse, where he headed for the small caricature of a standing man with the word 'Gentlemen' beside it. Descending the steps, he inspected the cubicles until he found one vacant, inserted a coin, and stepped inside. Thankfully, he slid home the bolt. Now he removed the moustache gently from his upper lip, being careful not to pull too rapidly. He'd been worried that a robust pull might remove some skin, and that would be a give-away. Moustache, glasses and panama hat all disappeared inside the roomy hold-all. Pity there was no mirror in there, he would have liked to reassure himself about the complete change in his appearance.

Time for the outside world again. He depressed the lever on the cistern, undid the door, and stepped out. Near the foot of the stairs was a contraceptive dispenser, and the lettering formed a kind of broken mirror. He looked at the bits of himself that appeared. That was Charlie Hurst, all right. No mistake. He went up the steps two at a time, and back out of the station into the sunlight. There were plenty of taxis around, and Charlie opened a door, instructing the driver to take him to Parkside South.

The hall porter was missing from his little cubbyhole when Mr. Patrick Owen passed through the foyer.

Just as well, he was in no mood for small talk anyway. Upstairs, he inserted his key and went into the flat, checking around carefully, as he always did. Mr. Owen didn't come near the place for days on end sometimes, and he'd heard terrible stories about the goings-on in vacant London properties. But there was no sign that anyone had been in. Satisfied, he threw the hold-all onto a chair, and walked over to the well-stocked bar. Here he selected a fine brandy, and poured himself a small measure.

"A nice tickle, Charlie my son" he muttered to himself. "Mud in yourn."

A small sip from the balloon glass, and he went across to a low glass-topped table, picking up the hold-all on his way.

"Now then, let's see what Father Christmas brought us."

Tipping the bag up, he emptied everything onto the table, pushing the pieces of disguise to the floor with distaste. Then he picked up one of the brown envelopes.

"Mr. J. E. Butcher," he read aloud, "Total Gross, fifty-one pounds sixty pence. National Insurance dah de dah, Income Tax—blimey—Pension Fund, Christmas Club—how many more things—Total Net, thirty-seven pounds eighteen. Thirty-seven pounds eighteen," he repeated. "They're having you on, Mr. Butcher old son. You'll never get rich working for that mob. You'd be better off selling programmes at the dog-track. Well, let's see if they got it right."

Charlie pulled out the folded notes and counted

them. At least Mr. J. E. Butcher had been given the right amount anyway. Or, rather, he would have been if a certain American tourist hadn't intervened. Let's see, what was the best way to arrange this lot. Could get in a terrible mess if he wasn't careful. We'll have the tens over there, the fives next door, and the ones in the middle. The change could go back in the hold-all, for now. Right then, who's next? Miss C. Butler. Ah, that's a bit more like it. Total Net, sixty-two pounds twelve. She was probably doing a turn for one of the bosses, or something.

The little piles of notes began to grow, and the floor became littered with torn brown envelopes. Finally he was finished. Charlie rummaged in the hold-all, to be quite certain one of the packets hadn't become lodged inside. He wasn't so concerned about the money, but the tell-tale envelope could put him inside, and Charlie Hurst wasn't the man to come unstuck over a detail like that. But the bag was empty, and he turned to the welcome task of counting the piles of money.

Five minutes later he sat back. He'd counted it all twice, and there was no mistake. Eighteen hundred and sixteen quid in notes, plus all the rubbish in the hold-all. Never mind about that, it was going to be a bleeding nuisance to get rid of anyway. Eighteen hundred quid, all in used notes, just for the asking. It had been a doddle right from start to finish, just the way that bloke Newton had promised. Imagine. If a man could do one of these a week life would be a doddle all round. Still, no use thinking like that. Jobs like this one didn't grow on trees. You had to have information, good information, and that was hard to come by.

Funny bloke, that Newton. Fancy just handing him this little lot on a plate. Didn't even want a share. Sign of good faith, he'd called it. Well, you'd have to admit, he'd been as good as his word. Every little detail was exactly the way he described it. No problems. Just walk in, pick up the money, walk out. Pity that silly old sod wanted to be Errol Flynn. Still, he didn't get hurt, as it happened, because he, Charlie, had kept his cool. He was pleased about that. It showed how far he'd come since his young days. He'd have left the old man half-dead then.

Once again he rifled happily at the pile of ten-pound notes. Lovely feel to a ten-pound note.

The telephone rang.

Charlie let it ring twice, three times, tempted to ignore it. Finally he picked it up. Jeremy Newton's voice said, "Ah, Patrick, is that you?"

No point in wondering how he managed to get hold of the ex-directory number.

"Yes," he confirmed.

"When you didn't turn up at the club, I guessed you'd gone off to that lunch-time party after all. Was I right?"

Charlie grinned to himself. Fly bugger, this Newton.

"Yes, I was there."

"Good do, was it? I mean, were you sorry you went?"

"Oh no," was the chuckling reply, "I was quite glad really."

Jeremy paused.

"I was wondering about the old man. I know you don't always hit it off with him. Was he awkward at all?"

So that was what he was after. He was afraid Charlie might have set about the old bugger. Well, he needn't have worried.

"No, no," he denied. "Nice as ninepence. No trouble at all."

There was no mistaking the relief at the other end of the telephone.

"Delighted to hear it. Well, I must be off. Got a meeting in a few minutes. Look, Patrick, perhaps you'll give me a ring next time you're in town. Love to have a nice long chat."

"I'll probably do that."

"Fine."

Newton said something else, and cut the connection. Charlie stared at the whirring receiver in his hand. What was that he said, Chow? Some kind of dog—big, fluffy-looking thing.

Chow?

He shrugged, and put the telephone down.

FOUR

Mara Newton sat in front of her dressing-table, stroking dutifully at her gleaming black hair, and counting. Forty-two strokes each side, my girl, morning and evening. That had been her mother's injunction, all those years ago. That, and regular washing with a mild soap. None of your fancy preparations, and above all, no hairdressers. Brush and wash, that was all there was to it. There had been many other edicts issued by her parents, most of which had been discarded along with woolly underwear, but there was no gainsaying the validity of this one. Her mother, now in her fifties, still looked ten years younger than any of her contemporaries, and this was largely due to her own crowning glory.

Forty-one, forty-two. Thank heavens that was over. Mara turned her head to admire the effect at each side of the triple mirrors. As she did so her hair danced gently, catching the late afternoon sun. Well, this wouldn't do, she must get dressed before Jeremy came home. It was awful, really, the way one had to live by the clock all the time. Rushing to complete all her chores before her luncheon commitment with the Conservative Ladies. Rushing up to London immediately coffee was served in order not to be late at a certain Bayswater hotel. Rushing back again on the four forty-five to give herself time for a bath and change before Jeremy got home.

Picking up her rumpled green suit from the bed, she began smoothing it before hanging it up. Increasingly, of late, she was beginning to wonder whether all this dashing about was worth while. The afternoon had not been a success. Tom Gardner was very sweet, of course, but he was beginning to get a little tiresome in some ways. Getting rather possessive, for one thing. Cross-examining her about her movements, which really, in the circumstances, was a bit presumptuous. There had been a shift in his attitude to their arrangements, as well. Whereas, when it all started, he had been eagerly grateful when she was able to arrange matters in order to see him, he was now becoming rather demanding, wanting to know why she couldn't manage such and such a day. It was very foolish of him to go on like that, and he'd picked the wrong girl. Mara found it quite irksome enough being expected to account to Jeremy for her movements, but at least he had the justification of his status. He was her husband, after all. If Tom thought she was going to start reporting all her movements to him as well, he had better think again.

Besides, she reflected as she opened the wardrobe door, it wasn't the same any more. No, that wasn't it. That was exactly the opposite of true. It was getting to be the same, and that was bad. The spontaneity was lacking these days. The whole business was getting to be rather routine. On top of that, he was actually expecting her to listen while he went on about his lack of progress within the company. Not exactly the kind of conversation a woman wants when she's—what was that marvellous expression of Aunt Thelma's—giving her all. That was it. Mara smiled at the quaintness of it. Damn right, though. A woman who was—clenched hand on bosom—giving her all ought not to be subjected to a lot of boring chat about the way the managing director had a down on the object of her favours.

Besides, Tom was getting a teeny bit flabby round the middle.

Lord, was that Jeremy's car turning in at the gate? Mara began to move smartly around the bedroom.

Jeremy left the car outside the front door. No point in putting it away, because he had a committee meeting at the golf club later that evening. Hallo, Mara's car was parked very close to the garage wall again. She'd managed to scrape the wing twice before doing that. Walking over, he checked to be certain she was actually clear of any obstruction this time. He put his hand on the bonnet to lean over, and removed it quickly. Engine must be running hot these days. Better have a look at the radiator before dinner.

Jeremy opened the front door of the house, and went in.

"Serving wench," he bawled.

It was his traditional greeting. Mara was half-way

down the stairs to meet him, pretty as a picture in that red wool thing.

"Lawks, Sir Jeremy, you did give me a start, sir. Will you take a stoop of mead?"

"No. But I'll take a bloody great gin and tonic, and a kiss from your rosy red lips," he commanded.

She came up to him, fluttering her eyelashes.

"Which would you like first?" she simpered.

Jeremy swept her up, and bit her ear. Then he smacked her on the rump.

"Gin-time. Come on."

In the drawing-room she mixed their drinks and handed one to him.

"Any big excitement today, darling?"

He took the glass, shaking his head.

"Same old routine. How about you? Been out?"

"Have I not," she replied, sitting down by an open window. "Luncheon with the Conservative Ladies, no less. I was a bit cross, actually. They had the cheek to ask if I'd consider being the secretary."

Jeremy grinned.

"Well, what's wrong with that? Too lazy, are we?"

Mara made a face. Men could be so worldly and knowledgeable about so many things, and yet be like babes in arms when it comes to distaff infighting.

"Not the point at all," she denied. "It's just that one doesn't do that sort of thing. Take office, I mean. That's for all these pushy little people, like the terrible woman married to that estate agent person. Or one of those town hall types. Those are the people who do all the work. I was quite affronted."

Her husband waved his glass.

"Probably having a go at you, old girl. Perhaps somebody thinks you need taking down a peg or two. Went on a bit, did it, your lunch?"

Mara was surprised.

"No. I got away quite early, as a matter of fact. Why do you ask?"

"Car engine's still warm," he replied, casually.

Christ. It was like being married to Sherlock Holmes.

"Oh. I expect it is. I popped over to Veronica's for a cup of tea."

"Ah. How is she?"

"Fine. Same as usual. I'm very fond of her, as you know, but I can't usually stand her for more than an hour at a time."

"M'm."

Jeremy seemed to lose interest, and Mara was relieved. The opposite was true, in fact. Jeremy was anxious not to show too much interest in Veronica Tate, now, or at any time. He'd always been strongly attracted to Mara's vivacious friend, with her outrageous clothes and ridiculous hair-styles. Most of the men in their circle were, but kept their real thoughts to themselves. If ever the opportunity came his way, Jeremy knew what he would do about it. In the meantime, Veronica was best kept out of the conversation, and relegated to her place as an odd friend of Mara's. Nothing more.

Glad of an opportunity to change the subject, Mara said, "When I was parking at the Bull today, I thought

I saw your friend's car. You know, that gangster type who was here the other week. It wasn't him, as a matter of fact, because I saw the driver later. But it reminded me of him. Did it come to anything in the end?''

Odd that Mara should raise the question of Charlie Hurst. Jeremy had been getting rather worried at not having heard from him. But he didn't care for the way she described him.

"I wish you wouldn't call him a gangster," he said shortly.

"But that's what you told me," she objected. "You told me he had a lot of cash he couldn't account for, and was looking for some way of getting it invested. Some way the income tax people couldn't query."

"That doesn't make him a gangster," insisted Jeremy.

"I don't know what else you'd call him," she pouted. "Perhaps you'd prefer 'crook'? Anyway, he looks like a gangster."

Mara welcomed the opportunity to talk about the mysterious Mr. Patrick Owen. She recalled with pleasure watching from the bedroom as he left that day, noting the ripple of muscles down the back of the well-cut suit. And his eyes. The way he'd looked at her when they were introduced had left her in no doubt as to his maleness. That was what had brought her to the window when he went out to his car.

Jeremy sighed. There was no reasoning with women.

"Mr. Owen didn't tell me how he came by his money," he told her. "But then, no client ever does. It's

none of my concern. Or yours," he added. A thought
struck him. "My God, I hope you're not saying this
kind of thing to anyone else? The Conservative Ladies,
for instance? 'Can't stop now, I'm expecting some of
my husband's gangster friends for dinner.'"

Mara chuckled richly.

"That would bring the pains on, wouldn't it? Don't
be silly, dear, of course not."

"Or Veronica?"

"Certainly not."

Especially not Veronica, thought Mara maliciously.
If Veronica ever got wind of an animal like Patrick
Owen, he would never make it to the car. Veronica
would have her teeth in his leg.

"Well, that's all right then. What's for dinner?"

After Mara had disappeared into the kitchen,
Jeremy went across to the window, staring out and
thinking. It had been a month now since his chat with
Charlie Hurst. An important chat, from his point of
view, and he'd hoped Charlie would think so too. Well,
he'd kept his word about that business with the wages.
Everything had gone like clockwork, exactly as he had
predicted. Charlie had walked off with eighteen
hundred quid, and there was no way the police could
ever trace the job to him. True enough, there had been
no commitment on Charlie's part, and he may simply
have decided to take the money and leave it at that.
There was no form of contract between them, not even
an understanding. It would simply mean that Jeremy
would have to start his search for a suitable partner all
over again. Pity, though. Because it also meant that

Jeremy had misjudged his man, and he didn't relish the thought that he might be slipping in that respect.

He ignored the ringing telephone, knowing that Mara would pick it up in the kitchen. It was probably only one of her friends, anyway.

"Jeremy?"

He heard her calling him, and went to the drawing-room door.

"You called?"

"Telephone," she pointed, from the kitchen. "It's your Peggy, from the office."

"Right, thanks."

Peggy had left early that day. Something about her mother being unwell. She was probably ringing to tell him she wouldn't be in the next day. Bloody nuisance.

"Hallo, Peggy," he said, into the extension.

"Oh, Mr. Newton, sorry to disturb you at home," said the familiar voice.

"That's all right. How did you find your mother?"

"Not too bad, thank you. The doctor's just left, and he says a couple of days' complete rest is what she needs."

Two days, groaned Jeremy inwardly.

"I see. You won't be coming in for a while, then?"

"Oh yes. I'll probably be an hour late in the morning, if that's all right. There'll be a friend coming in to see to her."

Then why telephone and bother me, he wondered.

"Well, that's good news. See you tomorrow then, Peggy."

"Don't go, Mr. Newton, I haven't told you why I

called, yet," she protested. "You were with a client when I left, so I couldn't speak to you. There was a telephone call. He was most insistent that you should know he'd tried to contact you. The name is not familiar to me, but he said you would know him. A Mr. Patrick Owen. Does that ring a bell, Mr. Newton?"

Oh yes, dear, that rings a bell. Loud and clear. All the way from Bow to St. Martin-in-the-Fields.

"Yes, it does, Peggy. A personal thing, nothing to do with the firm."

"Only he was very insistent, and I only just remembered, with my mother and everything."

"Perfectly all right. And I'm very glad you called. Thank you indeed, Peggy, and don't come in tomorrow until everything is settled at home."

She thanked him profusely and hung up.

Jeremy stood quite still, feeling exultant. It was going to happen. It was really going to happen. He was practically a millionaire, right at that moment. So Mr. Patrick Owen had called, had he? Then he had better call Mr. Patrick Owen back, that very evening.

This was a great day. A truly great day.

In the kitchen, Mara replaced the receiver with a thoughtful smile.

Charlie Hurst had been very busy since he relieved old Mr. Pettiford of all that cash. Life was not the simple matter of choice that his posh new friend Newton seemed to imagine. A man like Charlie could not announce that he'd decided to abandon his present way of living and take up some new venture. That was all right if you were some bleeding clerk in the town hall. Dear Sir, I hereby tender my resignation. Oh, why's that? Because I've had a better offer. Oh no. Charlie might be a big man, an important man, in his own world, but he couldn't do just what he liked, when he liked. There were too many people involved, people who were intimately concerned with his personal activities. Take the blokes who worked for him, for a start. Irish Tony and Mad Jimmy Evans. Couple of rough handfuls, them two. As long as Charlie was up and doing, and taking his nourishment, they'd give him no trouble. He was the guv'nor, the thinker, and they followed him. But not out of love. It wasn't a boys' club he was running. They followed him because he was strong and tough, and a lot quicker in the brain department. They lived well, saw plenty of the action their violent natures demanded, and were content. But if they thought things were going to change, their attitude would be very different. They'd either have to go it alone, which they weren't really up to, or find themselves a new leader, and that wasn't so easy. Either way, they'd be targets for any of Charlie's many enemies who kept their distance so long as he was around. No, they wouldn't like it if they knew what was in Charlies's mind.

And it didn't end with his own blokes. There was the important opposition, in the shape of King-size Saunders. That man had made a deal with Charlie not so long back that they would each try to keep out of the other's way. The deal was made from strength, not weakness. Each of them had enough to do running their own little empires, stamping on any signs of unrest, but always for profit, which was the name of the game. It made no sense for them to be always on the look-out for each other as well. Aggro for aggro's sake was for the street-fighter, the bar-room brawler. All right in its place, but men like Saunders and Hurst had reached a point in life where they didn't have to prove anything. They were both doing very nicely, thank you, and didn't need the expense and other inconvenience of a gang war. But that was between equals. If King-size got any wind of Charlie's intentions, he'd have his cutters out within the hour.

As if all that wasn't enough to occupy a man's mind, there were all the little people to consider. The mugs, the punters. Very respectful now, very careful how they spoke and behaved when Charlie Hurst was in view. Not that they fooled him for a minute. There was nothing they'd like better than to see him chopped, and he knew it, but there wasn't a man among them with the guts to raise a finger. That would change, too. Charlie had been very impressed with a nature film he'd seen on the telly once. It was about this lion who was getting a bit past it. Lions always fascinated him. Arrogant bastards, lions. Strolling about the jungle, doing what they liked, when they felt like it, and nobody to say boo to them. Bit like himself. And what happened to this one on the box, when he got a bit long in the tooth? Killed in a fight, was he, with some strong, young lion, one of his own kind? Not a bit of it. They had him, the punters. All the gutless bastards who'd kept out of his way while he was strong. Hyenas, vultures, even ants, they were the ones who had him. It was always like that, always would be. In Charlie's own case, it would be the street bookies, the prostitutes, and nobodies. The rubbish of his own particular jungle.

All this was going through Charlie's mind as he sat back in his Patrick Owen flat, a couple of hours after he locked old Pettiford in the cupboard. He was going to have to do a lot of thinking, a lot of planning, before he felt safe enough to accept Jeremy Newton's offer. Time was on his side, that was one good thing. As Newton had said, the scheme was good at any time. It wasn't one of these capers where the gold was being moved on a certain day, or anything like that. No pressure, and that was very important. Mr. Jeremy Newton could wait for his answer. Charlie had a lot to do, first.

It was four weeks later that he rang Jeremy's office.

FIVE

On the evening of the robbery, Charlie Hurst turned up in the saloon bar of the Crown at eight-thirty. He had told his two lieutenants to be there at half-past seven, with the deliberate intention of making them wait an hour. It reminded them who was boss, and they wouldn't question him.

"Hallo, Tony, Jim. Not late, am I?"

He looked at them challengingly. Both men shook their heads.

"Get you a drink, Charlie?" smiled Tony.

Irish Tony was twenty-six years old, a handsome, devil-may-care man, with an eye constantly on the look-out for a girl or a punch-up. It was all one to Tony which cropped up. He would sail into either with that indefinable élan which was his native heritage. Everybody liked him.

"Yes, right then. One whisky, four waters, you know how I have it."

This habit of Charlie's, of watering down good whisky like he did, had worried Tony at first. In his eyes, a real man drank his whisky as it came from the bottle, and the more of it he could sink the more of a man he was. But he'd come to learn the method in Charlie's seeming madness. Most of the real men would be stoned out of their minds in a few hours, useless to anybody. Charlie would still be packing away his mixture at six o'clock the following morning if he felt like it, still clear-headed, still able to think them out of trouble, still able to hold far more than his fair share of a brawl. A thinker-drinker, that was Charlie, Tony had decided, with his famous weakness for the invention of terrible rhymes.

He went up to the bar, and Mad Jimmy Evans leaned towards the newcomer.

"Any special plans tonight then, Charlie?"

He would have been surprised to know how much he had featured in Charlie's thoughts during the past few hours. Evans was not a large man, about five feet seven inches tall, and slimly built, but he was totally without fear in a punch-up. He had been known to attack three men, all by himself, and come out the winner, despite a few bruises. Fearless, yes, and vicious with it. A knife-artist was Jimmy Evans, and he would never hesitate to use his blade at the slightest provocation. He didn't award himself the title of 'Mad', and he would react violently if he heard anyone use it. But it was well justified. Unpredictable, moody, having Evans around was rather like sitting in a room full of gunpowder, waiting for someone to light a cigarette. Charlie Hurst was the only man who had ever been able to control him, and that was because Charlie had fathomed what made the little man tick. The violent side of his nature was deep inside him, always on the simmer. Every now and then it would boil over, and even Jimmy himself could never be certain when it would happen. He would pick fights in the wrong places, against the wrong opposition, frequently against even his own judgement. Charlie had gradually assessed his measure, and come up with a solution of his own. The secret was, not to wait until Jimmy erupted, but to draw off from his reserve of violence at controlled intervals. Make the man use it, when the time was ripe, and there was advantage to be had; then, he could be contained. Charlie had never confided to anyone how it came about that he seemed to be able to control this man whom everybody else had long decided was a murderous lunatic. If other people liked to think it was because Evans respected him, or was afraid of him, let them think it. The upshot was that Charlie always had available this walking bag of dynamite, and it was a powerful weapon in his armoury.

At the moment Mad Jimmy was in one of his safe periods, although even he didn't know that. Only the day before Charlie had sent him along to deal with a newsagent who was being difficult, and with specific instructions as to what needed doing. The newsagent was now in hospital, and the interior of his premises entirely destroyed by a berserk Evans using a fireman's axe. The axe had been a brainwave of Charlie's. He had worked it out that the physical exertion involved, and the enormous gratification of wreaking so much havoc with a heavy steel blade, would calm Jimmy down for the next few days. Certainly there was no tell-tale flicker in the eyes that now looked at him across the table.

He grinned.

"Thought we might go up the other end a bit later," he confided. "See if we can find some nice girls. Have a bit of a dance round. Sound all right to you?"

"Fine," agreed Jimmy. "We could do with a night off. It will be a night off, will it? I mean we're not going to have to speak to anybody, or like that?"

"No. Not tonight. Unless, of course, anybody gets naughty. But I don't think they will tonight, do you? Not if they read the papers."

Jimmy smiled reminiscently.

"Lovely, that was. They won't be getting their papers at that particular shop for a day or two, I reckon."

Tony came back with the drinks, and they relaxed for the evening.

The next day Charlie began to put in motion the plans for his eventual disappearance as Charles Hurst. Until then the shadowy figure of Patrick Owen had been no more than a useful gimmick. Owen had provided a temporary identity whenever Charlie needed one to further his relations with some bird or other, not to mention the premises essential to such cavortings. But since his talk with Jeremy Newton, he'd been giving a lot more thought to his alter ego. He had realised from the outset that the idea of Charlie Hurst as a millionaire was a non-starter. He'd never get a minute's peace, from the press, the law, or the hard men. Somebody would be at him, morning noon and night. It was no use having all that money if it brought you nothing but aggravation. The thing to do was to have Charlie Hurst drop out of society altogether. Just disappear. People would wonder, for a while, might even go looking for him. The police would give a few people some sleepless nights, because they would assume he'd been done in by the opposition and buried in some forest. But it would die down. There was nothing to tie Charlie to his present existence, no family to worry about. His father had disappeared when he was a child, and his mother had died when he was twenty-five. No one remained to mourn him, no one who would need to be let into the secret.

Charlie had decided to become Patrick Owen. It would all have to be legal, naturally. This deal with Newton wasn't going to be one of these cash-in-hand, no questions asked, transactions. It would involve banks, lawyers, signatures. And there had to be somebody real to give substance to the whole thing. The somebody was going to be Patrick Owen, and so Charlie knew he would have to change his name. He was very lucky in that regard, because he had a most imposing middle name that nobody knew anything about. The reason it was unknown was because Charlie had found himself in so many fights over it as a small boy that he'd learned to keep it to himself. It was all his mother's doing. She had always been a great admirer of the actor, Basil Rathbone. When Charlie was born she had resisted the name Basil because that could refer to anybody, or nobody. Rathbone was different, and an astonished registrar in the town hall found himself entering a birth certificate for Charles Rathbone Hurst, with the last two names hyphenated, and that would be how his name would appear in the list of applications. Probably nobody bothered to read the list anyway, but Charlie was not the man to take unnecessary chances. If some nosey copper, or newspaper bloke happened to take an interest in people who wanted to change their names, they would never in a month of Sundays associate Rathbone-Hurst, Charles, with Charlie Hurst of Clapham.

That was his first step along the road, the end of which would also see the end of his present existence. He was surprised at how easy it all was. Nobody asked him any questions as to why, nobody took his fingerprints. There was about as much fuss as there would be booking a seat for the theatre. It was all very routine to them, practically boring, judging by the amount of interest anybody showed. It would take time, he was told, he would be notified in due course, and so forth. Simple.

Encouraged by this early success, his next move was to open a bank account. There was no trouble there, either.

"Your occupation, Mr. Owen?"

He'd expected that one.

"Investments. The City, you know."

The assistant manager of the branch wrote down 'Investments Counsellor'. Charlie need not have been concerned about his lack of a black jacket and striped trousers image. This was a West End branch, and the assistant manager was well acquainted with an extraordinary variety of types who derived their livelihood from the quirky machinations of the City.

"If you could give me just one name, as a reference, Mr. Owen?"

"Rathbone-Hurst, Charles Rathbone-Hurst. That's with a hyphen, of course."

"Of course."

Charlie handed over two hundred pounds to get his account started, and went back out into the street. Better and better.

If he had been an impatient man he would have put through a call to Jeremy Newton's office after the first few days. But the whole venture was too important to be rushed. Mr. Patrick Owen was so far only a name in a couple of people's registers. There had to be more to him than that. Clothes, for one thing. Owen had none of his own, only whatever Charlie Hurst happened to be wearing whenever he turned up at the flat. What sort of stuff would he wear, this Owen? Charlie had always tried to keep himself looking well turned out, but Mr. Owen was going to be a man of property. A Savile Row man. Charlie hailed a taxi.

It was just as well he had allowed himself some time, he realised. True enough, there were some premises with ready-made suits, but he was quickly given to understand these were really for foreigners who hadn't much time in London, but wanted something with the Savile Row label. And so he submitted himself to the tape-measure, and agreed to report back for a first fitting in ten days' time.

He was getting into the spirit of the thing now. There were shirts to be acquired, shoes, ties. Charlie knew when he was out of his depth, and so he described the materials of the three suits he'd ordered and let the salesman guide him from there. Mind you, he reflected, there were some right liberty-takers about. Eighteen quid for a tie wanted a bit of swallowing, but then, Mr. Patrick Owen would not be the man to quibble over price.

Gradually, the flat at Parkside South began to assume the appearance of a place someone lived in. There were clothes in the wardrobes for the first time, and linen in the drawers. The *Financial Times* was pushed through the letter-box each day. Mr. Patrick Owen would want to keep in touch with developments on the market front. He even acquired two credit cards, and used them for purchases connected with the flat. Charlie had always enjoyed the time he spent at Parkside South, but now he was beginning to feel really at home in the place. In fact, if he wasn't careful, he realised, he was going to become resentful of the time spent elsewhere, and this he would have to guard against. He must never lose sight of the fact that the Patrick Owen world was a dream-world, a fantasy, and no more than that as yet. The real world, the one where Charlie Hurst lived, with all its dangers and stresses, was outside. That was the one that mattered, until the time came for the great change. If he relaxed his vigil out there, permitted himself to daydream, then the hyenas and the vultures would be picking over his entrails in no time. He was under no illusions about that.

So far so good. Mr. Owen now had a proper address, his own clothes, a properly equipped kitchen, mail being delivered, and credit status. Mr. Owen was beginning to take shape.

The irony of it was not lost on Charlie. Here he'd gone to all this trouble of renting the place in the first instance so that he could have a little hide-away to take his playmates to, and now that it was beginning to look lived-in for the first time he had to cease activity in that direction. Fond as he was of the opposite sex, Charlie was under no illusions about them, or his ability to control them if they got out of hand. If a woman began to get interested in Patrick Owen, he could find himself in trouble in no time. In Charlie's world it went without saying that you never discussed work with women, not even with wives or mothers. Sooner or later one of them would drop a man in it, and then the balloon was up. They didn't mean any harm, as often as not, but they couldn't stop their tongues from wagging.

There was only one major problem, and that was that he couldn't permit people to put a face to the name Patrick Owen. Not Charlie Hurst's face. That was going to change, only in small ways, but they should be significant. Owen would have a moustache and glasses, and a Tony Curtis haircut. The glasses and the haircut were easy enough, and could be put into effect at short notice. The moustache was another matter entirely, and would take two to three weeks to grow into the shape and luxuriance Charlie had decided on. As a stop-gap measure he had purchased several examples from a theatrical shop, and tried these in front of the mirror until he found the one he wanted. He would keep out of the public eye as much as possible, while compelled to wear the stage moustache, but it had a convincing appearance and would certainly meet his needs while his own whiskers were growing.

All these things took time, and it was all time that he had to take away from his usual activities. What a man would normally accomplish in a week or ten days was taking Charlie Hurst weeks to achieve. He could not afford to be missing too often, or for too long, from places where people normally expected him to be.

As it was, he'd had one close encounter already, which had made him even more careful than usual. He'd decided to buy a few decent cups and saucers, in place of the mugs so far used for drinking coffee at the Owen establishment. Undecided where to obtain such items, he settled for Harrods. He'd seen the women out shopping, flashing their carrier bags with the Harrods imprint on the outside. It certainly would do no harm to the future Mr. Owen's image if the odd Harrods bag was to be seen, dropped carelessly to one side.

Charlie made his purchases, and was on his way out of the main entrance, when a voice said, "Hallo, Charlie. What are you doing up here, then?"

He turned to look into the unwelcome face of Johnny Barker.

Forcing a smile to his lips, he replied, "Oh hallo, Johnny. Bit of shopping, you know."

Johnny looked puzzled.

"Wonders'll never cease," he marvelled. "Never had you down as a shopping man, Charlie."

But Charlie had regained his composure in those few seconds. Looking around conspiratorially, he whispered, "Ah no, not me. Mugs' game, shopping. This is a bit different, you see, John. There's this bird, and I'm doing all right, if you follow me. Thought I'd take her a little present. I tell you, one look at this label, and she'll practically tear me shirt off."

An elaborate explanation would have been regarded with scepticism, but the introduction of the sex motive was accepted without question.

"Lucky sod. Say no more," winked Johnny. "Hasn't got a friend, has she?"

"Oh yes," agreed Charlie, "they're twins actually. But I need 'em both myself."

"I should cocoa," chortled his inquisitor. "All right for some. See you down there Saturday, then?"

"They'll probably carry me down there, between 'em."

"Lucky sod," repeated Johnny. "Well, ta ta, then."

"So long."

Johnny Barker went about his business, and Charlie sighed with relief. He'd thought once or twice he might be making too much of a mystery about the simple things, but this encounter only reinforced his original ideas. There was no such thing as being too careful, not when you were on a job as important as this.

He waved to a taxi, and had himself driven away in the opposite direction from Parkside South, just in case

Johnny happened to be watching. Half a mile away he got out, and took a second cab back to the flat.

There had been no other mishaps of that kind, and when he had run into Barker the following Saturday the only reference to their meeting had been a knowing wink.

But gradually the skeleton of Mr. Patrick Owen was fleshing out, and one day Charlie sat alone in the flat, looking around with great satisfaction, and checking over his various mental lists to see whether there was anything else which ought to be done before he gave the signal to Jeremy Newton.

One of the subjects he'd been dwelling on during the previous month had been Newton himself. He didn't know the man, after all, didn't know how far he could really trust him. Because, at the end of their particular road, when the big prize was on the table, the only person who could possibly put Charlie Hurst and Patrick Owen in the same box would be Newton. Charlie admitted to himself that he had no reason to distrust the man. After all, it was as much in Newton's own interest to keep mum as it was Charlie's. Just the same, that man certainly would have an edge, and Charlie didn't care to have him in that position. While they were doing what they were going to do, he'd have to try to see whether there wasn't some little thing he could get on the other man. Not to hurt him with it. Just to have it, and make certain Newton was aware that he had it.

Still, that was for later. The thing now was to give the man a bell.

Newton wasn't in his office when they answered, and Charlie talked to some girl who seemed to know what she was doing. Yes, she assured him, she would see to it without fail that Mr. Newton had his message. Yes, she quite understood that it was urgent, and he could take her personal guarantee that it would be done.

Hours later, Charlie looked at the clock. Well, if that girl had done her stuff, Jeremy Newton ought to be on the blower in the next hour or so.

The bell startled him out of his reverie. Charlie picked up the new red-leather receiver.

"Mr. Owen?"

It was Newton's voice.

"Yes," confirmed Charlie. "Is that who I think it is?"

"I hope so." Newton sounded very cheerful. "I think we ought to meet for a chat, don't you?"

"Sounds reasonable," agreed Charlie.

SIX

George Blandford yawned, then jerked himself upright guiltily. He ought never to have had that second brandy after lunch, but dammit, it was an occasion for celebration. All the to-ing and fro-ing of the last few hectic days had put a strain on them all, but on no one more than himself. Other people had to produce revised figures, estimates and so forth, on the basis of each new development, and that meant plenty of midnight oil in all departments. But when the final decision was taken, they were finished, their part was done. It was the poor old company secretary who had to knock it all into shape, reduce it to terms that even the most bumbling of the name-only directors could understand at tomorrow's Board meeting. Well, after tomorrow it would all be public news. There'd be plenty to do, naturally, but the secrecy would be taken out of it. George would be able to delegate the routine matters to other people, instead of having to deal with every detail himself.

There was a tap at the door.

"Come in."

Miss Freed came noiselessly into the room, clutching a pile of paper against her bony chest.

"Is that it, Miss Freed? All done, are we?"

She laid the papers beside him on the desk, nodding.

"It's all finished, Mr. Blandford."

Good old Freed. George didn't know what he would have done without her during these past weeks. All that overtime, missed lunches, and never a word of complaint.

"Any spoiled copies?" he demanded.

"A few. I put them through the shredder myself."

"Good. And you've kept one set for your own file outside, have you?"

It was a trick question. Miss Freed looked horrified.

"Why no, I haven't. I didn't think you wanted me to. You said you wanted every scrap of paper on your own desk."

Blandford was satisfied. He oughtn't to test the old girl like that, but there was no elbow-room for mistakes at this juncture.

"And my hand-written stuff?" he persisted.

"At the bottom of the pile."

Miss Freed was slightly miffed at being cross-examined. You'd have thought she'd been with Mr. Blandford long enough for him to feel able to rely on her. Of course, he had been under a lot of strain, with this takeover and everything.

The intercom buzzed at the 'Chairman' position.

"You there, George?"

"Yes, sir."

"Anyone with you?"

"Miss Freed is here, sir."

"Ah, yes. Look George, could you hang on for a few minutes tonight? Just like a final word, after the staff have left."

"Yes of course, sir."

Blast. He'd been hoping to catch the five-ten for the first time in weeks. Miss Freed smiled her sympathy.

"Good. I'll give you a call."

The Chairman broke the connection.

"I can stay on if you like, Mr. Blandford. I'm in no hurry to get away."

Amazing woman. Blandford was lucky to have her, and he knew it.

"No need, thanks all the same. The work is done. I'm sure there won't be anything I can't cope with."

Miss Freed didn't press the point. It was her night for the flower-arranging class, and she'd missed the previous week as it was.

"Perhaps I'd better leave the copier on, just in case you need it. You will switch it off before you leave, won't you, Mr. Blandford. It tends to overheat, you know."

"Eh? Oh, the copier. Yes. Thank you. No, I won't forget it." He wasn't really listening. He was wondering what Jessica was going to say. His last words to her that morning had been an unconditional guarantee that he would not miss dinner in the evening. He knew what her reaction would be, and he didn't want to listen to it. "Before you leave, Miss Freed, would you mind telephoning Mrs. Blandford for me? Explain the situation. Tell her I'll be home as quickly as I can."

"Yes, of course. Well, if you're sure you don't want me to stay, I'll be off after that."

He looked at the clock. A quarter to five already.

"Good Lord, is that the time? Yes, yes by all means. And thank you for all this."

He patted at the papers beside him.

"Not at all. Good night, Mr. Blandford."

Poor man. She seemed to spend half her time explaining to his wife why he wasn't going to make one social appointment or another. It was a good job she and Mrs. Blandford had met a couple of times, otherwise the woman might think—oh dear. Miss Freed coloured slightly as she closed the door behind her.

At ten past five the buzzer rang again. Blandford noted the time. He should be just moving out of Victoria now.

"Sir?"

"Come in, George."

He gathered up his vital papers and went along to Sir Edward's room. The great man beamed at him, evidently well pleased with life. Well, he had every reason to be. This takeover was a great day for them all.

"That's all the stuff there, is it?"

"Yes, sir. Thought you might just like to look at it in its final form."

"Ah."

The Chairman leaned over the desk, holding out a piece of paper.

"You can chuck that lot away, George. Read this."

Chuck it away? What the devil—

Blandford put his papers down and took the extended note. His face dropped. Then he read it again, and tried to speak, but no words came.

Sir Edward chuckled.

"Thought that would make you sit up."

"But this is half as much again as Associated."

"Exactly. That, George, is what our American friends call an offer we can't refuse. We'd be bloody mugs to try."

Blandford's mind was still racing.

"This is genuine, of course? I mean there's no question of some elaborate hoax? This is only a piece of paper, after all."

Sir Edward did not take exception to his caution.

"That was handed to me personally half an hour ago, by Jack Houghton himself."

Well, that ended the matter. Blandford adjusted his thinking, as he'd had need to do so often in the past weeks.

"My figures are useless. I can never get all this lot revised by tomorrow's meeting. Half a day's typing at least, even after the drafts are done. And they'll take hours."

The chairman nodded.

"Aware of all that. Don't worry about it. Nobody's going to argue about back-up papers when they hear that. What you can do, George, is the summary sheet, can't you?"

"Well, it would be a rough job, sir. Nothing to back it up, if there are questions."

The seated man waved.

"Don't worry about questions. If any of those dunderheads start trying to earn their fees for a change, I'll stamp on 'em. It's the bottom line that counts tomorrow, George. Nothing else. What about the summary?"

"Oh, yes. I can get it done. Have to."

"Good. Keep that in your own hands, George. No copies, not even for me."

"Right, sir. Well, I'd better get on with it. I'll tell the security people not to lock me in."

The Chairman shook his head.

"Don't want you stopping on here. Might cause speculation. Don't want people putting two and two together. Prefer it if you went home and did it there."

Jessica would be delighted, reflected George. Especially with him locked in his study until bedtime.

"No trouble at all, sir." Then he added, "Well, I knew tomorrow was going to be a great day, but I had no idea just how great."

"Neither has anyone else. Only you and I know about this. It has to remain that way until the meeting. If any of the others happen to ring you at home, not a word."

"Naturally not, sir."

He got away soon afterwards, and was able to make the six-ten from Victoria. It was to be many hours later that he went thankfully to bed.

The first indication of trouble was the noise of excited voices, and feet pounding on the stairs. Blandford stirred irritably, and looked at the bedside clock. Six-fifteen. Hell's teeth, he didn't have to be up for another thirty minutes yet. Why didn't Jessica control those children in the mornings?

There was heavy banging at the door.

"Daddy, Daddy. Come quick. Burglars. We've got burglars."

The excited voice of his eldest son penetrated the fog of his mind. What was the boy on about? Burglars? Ridiculous. Place was burglar-proof.

"Daddy, wake up. Come on."

It must be something, or they wouldn't dare wake him. They knew what he was like before he'd had his coffee. Struggling out of bed, he reached for his dressing-gown, and went downstairs. The place seemed to be alive with children, and then he remembered that Angus had a couple of chums from school staying the night.

Somebody had been in all right. Things were turned over, drawers emptied. He went into the study. Suppose his papers had been stolen? But they were all right, merely scattered around as the intruder searched for valuables. George Blandford felt quite weak with relief.

Jessica appeared with a cup of coffee.

"I wasn't going to wake you without this," she greeted. "Sorry about the kids."

He nodded, sipping gratefully at his drink.

"Well, this is a fine mess. Had a chance to see what's missing?"

"Not really. Some cash from the kitchen, about seven or eight pounds. I haven't had a chance to look properly yet. But why didn't anything work? All these marvellous gadgets we've got? They cost enough."

George was wondering the same thing. Electronic seals, photo-electric cells, nothing seemed to have worked. It was not until later that he found the main electricity supply in the garage had been cut off.

Jeremy Newton left home for the office very early that morning. Mara did not bother to get up to see him off. Normally quite dutiful in such matters, she really couldn't see why she should stir herself two hours earlier than usual. Jeremy's photography did not normally disturb their weekday life, being confined as a rule to the weekends. But if he wanted to go dashing off to photograph the Thames at this ungodly hour, well he could jolly well get on with it.

City-based photography enthusiasts had long since formed themselves into a club, and one of the great Fleet Street newspapers had obligingly given them the use of a few square feet in the basement, part of which was partitioned off as a darkroom. No one took any particular notice of the tall fair man who appeared in the early morning, waving his camera. Most photographers were known to be slightly crazy anyway, and the amateurs were the worst of the lot.

In the letter-box was a square envelope addressed to J. Newton Esq., and the tall fair man lifted it out, feeling the hard outline of the plastic cartridge inside. Then he went into the dark room and set to work. He was soon congratulating himself on his own wisdom in having given Charlie Hurst such an expensive camera to work with. Charlie was no photographer, that much was quickly evident, but it was almost impossible to do wrong with that ingenious little box. With mounting excitement, he began to examine the results.

At six o'clock that evening, a tall dark-haired man was sitting in the waning sunshine on a bench on the Embankment. People passed by in two steady streams. One stream headed for the tube station and home, those who had worked later than most. The other stream came from the opposite direction, early starters in the search for a night out in the capital. For Charlie Hurst, they all had one thing in common. They were all mugs, punters, of no more significance than the fat pigeons who strutted impertinently a few feet away from him. In the telephone box behind him a girl was chattering away to some admirer, with the door open, so that her friend could join in the conversation and offer her suggestive interpretations of everything that was said. Charlie looked at his watch, and scowled, wondering how much longer the two little darlings would be. Phones were for messages, not bleeding chat-parties. There ought to be a law.

The thought of the law brought his mind back to the newspaper lying beside him on the bench, ruffling gently in the slight breeze. No reference to the burglary at the home of Mr. George Blandford, City Gent. Nor had there been all day. Charlie had bought every edition of both the London evening papers from the mid-day onwards, and hadn't found so much as a two-line item. Funny, that was. You'd think it would get a little mention. True enough, it wasn't what you'd call the crime of the century. He'd only taken about fifty quid's worth of small items, just to make it look good, and those had found a new home at the bottom of the river. Charlie Hurst wasn't going to have his collar felt through being greedy over a couple of trinkets. No, it wasn't exactly the big-time, none of your million pound raids. Still, he was a well-known man, this Blandford. You'd have thought they could spare him a bit of room. Charlie felt slightly aggrieved that his debut into the world of burglary should receive such short shrift. It didn't enter his head that George Blandford had not reported what had happened. To him it was an automatic action. When a punter got himself done, he hollered for the law, and screamed bloody murder. That was what he paid all those taxes for, wasn't it? More fool him. Charlie had no way of knowing that George Blandford, once satisfied that his losses were small, had reasons of his own for not wishing it to be bruited about that he had been burgled. Least said, the soonest mended, Blandford had decided. His name would appear in the newspapers later that day, but in the City pages, and that was quite enough. He wanted no cross-reference to the pages dealing with home news. People might wonder about the wisdom of entrusting documents to a chap who allowed himself to be burgled at such an inconvenient time. Why, even Sir Edward himself—George had shuddered, swallowed some more coffee, and called the family together for a few stern words.

The man on the Embankment had no way of knowing any of this, and was left to wonder. Nearly ten past six. How long were those two silly cows going to be

on that phone? He glared in their direction. The one
holding the door nudged her friend, who looked over at
Charlie, sniffed and turned her back.

A small boy sauntered along, a heavy wooden tray
strapped around his shoulders.

"Feed the pigeons," he called, "lovely bird-seed."

Well, why not? Better than listening to those other
birds on the phone.

"Here you are, son."

The boy stopped, lifted a small white bag from his
tray, and held it out.

"There you are. All top quality. Twenty-five pee."

Charlie looked at him in astonishment.

"Twenty-five?" he echoed. "Your name's not
Rothschild, is it?"

The young salesman didn't know what he meant,
and shook his head.

"No," he denied.

"Well, keep this up, son. It will be, one day."

He handed over the money, and opened the bag.
One or two of the nearer pigeons sized up the situation
at once and pattered across to him. He flung the seed
out in an arc, and soon there was a large flock of the
birds, pecking and swaggering in front of him. In a
couple of hours, he reflected, the sun would go down,
and they would all disappear, to roost on the tall
buildings lining the river. They weren't ones to stop up
late, not pigeons weren't. Me neither, not tonight, he
decided. Quite late enough last night, thank you, and
not able to catch up during the day. Well not much,
anyway. After the disappointment of the lunch-time

papers, Charlie had nothing to do until six o'clock. He decided to while away a few hours in the cinema. Of course, he would go and pick on a gangster picture, wouldn't he? Gave young kids all the wrong ideas, they did. Look at the two geezers in this one. 'Life of Riley'. Rushing about, waving shooters, birds lying down waiting for 'em, everywhere they went. Course, they'd get their faces blown off at the end of the picture, but the kids never thought about that part. Not that Charlie ever found out how it ended. He was asleep by the end of the first reel.

"We'll have to shift a bit, Sandra. He said a quarter to seven, outside the Odeon."

"Oh, did he. Well, he'll have to bleeding wait. I'm not running in these shoes."

"Oh, come on, Sand."

Charlie realised the two girls had vacated the telephone box. Six-fifteen. Well, it wasn't his fault. He'd been here on time. He just hoped Jeremy hadn't given up, that was all. The phone rang in the empty box. Charlie winked at the nearest pigeon, a huge bird with a mauve chest.

"It's your birthday, son. Here."

He put the packet down in front of the waiting bird, and went into the telephone box.

"Is that you, Mr. Owen?"

Jeremy Newton's voice sounded anxious.

"It's me," he confirmed. "Phone's been engaged ever since I got here. How did we do? Can you talk at your end?"

"Oh yes," said Jeremy confidently. "I'm in a box,

too. If anybody does listen they can't trace who we are. Any trouble last night?"

"No. It was a right doddle. How did I do with me little pictures?"

The man at the other end laughed.

"Oh, I think we might say you did very well. Better than I really expected."

"Why's that, then?"

"We all knew that Associated would be making a bid. All I was after was to find out how much, if we could. It could have been on the low side, you see. Not really worth our while."

Charlie hoped all this wasn't going to get too technical for him. All he really wanted to know was how much they scored.

"And was it, then? On the low side?"

"No. It was anything but. A very handsome offer indeed. But that wasn't the whole of it. Do you remember one piece of paper that was different from the rest? Hand-written note?"

Charlie recalled it at once.

"Yes. I remember it. Didn't make any sense. I almost didn't bother with it. Only about two lines. Still, you said you needed it all."

There was a pause. The listening man had no way of telling that Newton was adjusting to the terrifying idea that Charlie had considered not bothering with the most vital document of all. The voice came back.

"Well, just let's all be thankful you did bother. That was a last-minute bid from a Belgian combine. It was twenty per cent higher than the Associated offer."

"That was better still then, was it? For us, I mean."

"I should just say it was. I may as well tell you, it was all I could do to stop myself."

Charlie was mystified.

"Stop yourself doing what?" he asked.

Jeremy laughed.

"From selling everything I possess. Putting every farthing I could raise on the lucky number. With that information, I could have made half a million today. Thank God I was able to talk some sense into myself."

That part made sense. Charlie recalled their original conversation when they'd discussed horse-racing.

"You mean you might have made a fortune today, but the men with the questions would have been around tomorrow? Like the big bookies?"

"Exactly. Just like the big bookies. So I played it safe. Took what looked like a fair gamble. Guess how much we took home?"

That 'we' sounded nice.

"Go on then."

"Fourteen—thousand—pounds."

Jeremy spaced the words out carefully. Charlie whistled his appreciation.

"Are you telling me that I'm worth half of that? Seven grand?"

"I am," came the reply. "Not bad for taking a few photographs, is it? How do you feel?"

"I feel great," Charlie endorsed. "When's the next one?"

This brought a brief chuckle.

"Not just for a while. We mustn't go too fast. There's

no point in our taking all these precautions if we're going to draw attention to ourselves in the end. We'll leave it a week or two. I'll be in touch."

It all seemed a bit off-hand to Charlie.

"Well yes, I suppose so. You be very careful with my seven grand."

"Wouldn't dream of touching it, old boy," he was assured. "We're going to need that for our next little—shall I say 'investment'?"

"Soon as you say the word. Don't go making yourself ill, or anything. Can't have anything happening to you."

"That goes double for you. Well, I'll call you in a while, at the flat."

"Right."

Charlie replaced the receiver and walked outside to look at the river. It was all going to happen. He could feel it. Charlie Hurst was going to be a millionaire. He winked at a trio of girls who were walking towards him, arms linked. They all put on lofty expressions and turned their heads away.

A policeman regarded him with a piercing stare.

My Gawd, thought Charlie.

If only you knew.

SEVEN

June was a good month that year. The sun had arrived in earnest in mid-May, and except for a heavy downpour of rain during the last two days of that month there had been continuous sunshine now for almost five weeks. The important matter of keeping cool in the city was occupying people's time and attention. Ice-cream factories were on permanent overtime, and in the public houses landlords had an uphill struggle to meet the demand for cold beer. Supplies were not on the premises long enough for them to be chilled adequately, and the heavy delivery lorries were an increasingly familiar sight on the streets. As always, the hot weather brought its complications. The lawn tennis at Wimbledon had been marred by some unusually violent displays of temperament. At Lord's, the test match had been enlivened by the trio of ladies from FEM, the Female Emancipation Movement. It was their contention that since it had become increasingly acceptable for male spectators to sit bare to the waist, it was no more than simple equality for female spectators to enjoy the same privilege. This they demonstrated in front of the pavilion, to the delight of the crowds, the dismay of the umpires, and apoplexy of the members.

These, and the more usual hot-weather lunacies, such as the inevitable fountain-bathers in Trafalgar Square, kept the gentlemen of the press well supplied with trifles to titillate their readers.

Unfortunately not all the consequences of the heat were so light-hearted. There was trouble in the tenement districts, where overcrowding, always a flashpoint, was accentuated by the relentless sun. Sporadic outbursts of violence brought ever more pressure on the overworked police, and tempers were seldom far from high.

The criminal fraternity, too, were far from immune to the heat. There had already been one major invasion of a Soho street by East End gangsters, who had no particular reason for what they did. It was simply that increasing discomfort and irritation demanded an outlet, and in their case there was only one solution. Shirt-sleeves and the new light-weight trousers were the order of the day for the police, already showing signs of the strain inseparable from undermanning and continuous overtime.

One particular lunch time Irish Tony elbowed his way into the crowded saloon bar of the Crown, looking around for Mad Jimmy Evans. Having spotted his man, he made drinking signs with his hands, and ordered from the sweating barman. Then he put the glasses on a tray and made his way across the barroom. Evans sat alone, although there were empty chairs at the table. Everyone always gave the little man a wide berth at the best of times, but in this heat it was even more sensible to keep away from him.

"What ho then, Jim boy."

Jimmy grunted.

"Who's all that booze for, then? Queen's popping in, is she?"

Tony set out the drinks, grinning.

"Have to buy her own, if she does. These are ours, me boy. Can't keep on traipsing up and down there every five minutes."

"Ah."

They sipped at their drinks. Tony smacked his lips and looked around.

"Bleeding hot," he offered.

Evans did not feel like talking. He was feeling the heat, like everyone else, but in his case the problem went deeper. Things had been quiet for too long. It had been weeks since they went out on any kind of scrimmage, and Mad Jimmy was not the man to flourish under inactivity.

"M'm," he muttered.

Tony was not discouraged.

"You shoulda come up there last night. It was good. They had this girl doing a little act, know what I mean? Disgusting it was, really. Good though. Right laugh. Where'd you get to?"

"Bed," was the brief reply.

Mad Jimmy had a very different idea of a good night out. The handsome Irishman went his own way on those occasions. Tony tried again.

"Charlie been in, then?"

That brought a more positive reaction.

"No, he bleeding hasn't."

Hallo, thought Tony, feeling a bit cross, are we? He was one of the few people who could manage to keep on the right side of the little man facing him. Not that Tony was afraid of him. Tony was afraid of nobody, except maybe Charlie Hurst himself, and even then not always. But he and Evans were on the same firm, and you don't quarrel with your own. That would be just plain silly. The way Mad Jim had reacted to Charlie's absence might mean something, might not. There hadn't been a lot going on lately, just the usual Friday and Saturday collections, and nobody had even given them any argument about those. Mind you, the cost of living was going up all the time, it said so in the papers. They were still collecting the same money they had been for a long time past. Perhaps it was time they put their prices up as well. Everybody else did. Look at the cost of those drinks just now. Perhaps he ought to mention it to Charlie. Pick his time, of course. You had to be very careful how you spoke to Charlie, sometimes. Especially if he thought you might be giving him an argument. Not that he'd been hard to live with, lately. Far from it. Good as gold, Charlie was. Bit too good, perhaps. Maybe that was why Jimmy was a bit out of sorts. Meantime, where was Charlie?

"I spect he'll look in," he suggested.

"I hope so," grumbled Evans. "I tell you, Tony, I'm getting a bit restless."

Oh dear. That usually meant bad news for somebody.

"Oh yes," Tony tried to keep his voice light. "What's up then?"

Mad Jimmy looked around him. A tall man, who happened to be looking quite innocently in their direction, turned hastily away.

"Getting a bit restless," repeated Jimmy. "What are we supposed to be doing—you and me, I mean?"

Tony was puzzled.

"Doing? Why, we're sitting here having a coupla nice jars, that's what we're doing. How d'you mean, like?"

"That's what I mean," replied Evans, scowling. "And what were we doing this time yesterday, tell me that? I'll tell you that. The same. We've been doing the same for bleeding weeks. Getting on my wick."

The Irishman shook his head. He thought he knew what the other was driving at, but he wanted to be sure.

"What's wrong with it?" he queried.

"I'll tell you, my son, if you don't know. It's all wrong, that's what. There's you, and here's me. Hard men, we're supposed to be. People mind their Ps and Qs when we walk in. But we never do anything. All we do is take our little walk round at the end of the week, pick up our money. We hand it over to Charlie, and he gives us our wages."

"Not bad wages though. Three hundred apiece every week, plus a bit extra now and then if we do a bit of overtime. What d'you want, Jim, more money?"

Evans snorted in disgust.

"Money," he scoffed. "Charlie looks after us, I'm

not complaining."

"Well, what then?"

"Hard men are supposed to be hard, sometimes. You have to remind people. And what do we do? Sit on our asses all day, boozing. We're like a couple of bleeding landlords, living off the rent. Life is too quiet. And you know what happens if you let things slide. One day, you go into a car park, there's people waiting to speak to you. They've been watching you, watching how easy it is to make a few bob. Watching you get fat, careless. When you come out of the hospital, there's new faces. Not so easy to shift 'em, once they're in."

It was true, and no one knew it better than Irish Tony. That was exactly how he'd got his own start, years before. It was a pity it had to be raised, but he couldn't argue with the sense of what Jim was saying. Mad or not, when he was on the rampage there was nothing wrong with Jim in the think department.

"So, what are you thinking of doing about it?" he asked softly.

He'd been careful to say 'you', not 'we'.

Evans dropped his voice even lower.

"Been thinking of going for a nice ride in the car one night."

"Oh yes." This was going to be bad news for somebody. "Anywhere special?"

"Out Epping way. Little club out there, very nice. Mate of ours runs it."

The only club that Tony could recall was run by a man who was no mate of anybody's, but especially theirs. His name was King-size Saunders.

"Smokes very long fags, does he, this mate?" he asked carelessly.

"Very long," agreed Evans, with a savage grin. "Oh yes, quite long. Fancy a ride, do you?"

Tony pursed his lips, thinking. There was a lot of truth in what Mad Jim was saying. It wasn't good for blokes like them to remain inactive. They were a bit like boxers, or racehorses, in that respect. They had to have regular work-outs to keep in trim. You didn't find boxers sitting around in pubs, letting everybody think they were boxers. They had to get in the ring every now and then, remind people. Show they could still do it. And, he realised, when you carried that a bit further, the ones who did sit around in the pubs were the ones who hadn't got it any more. He'd seen a few of those, too. Has-beens.

Yes, there was sense in Evans' complaints. The time had probably come when they should be doing something about it. The only question was, what? He wasn't at all sure that trying to carve up one of Saunders' places was the right answer. Not at all sure. Saunders was an important man, as important as Charlie Hurst, in his own way. If they were going to have a go at him, it would have to be with Charlie's approval. It wasn't something you went and did just because you felt like it.

Where was Charlie, anyway? He ought to be here, taking part.

"I'll tell you, Jim," he said earnestly. "I don't know. I really don't. How would it be if we took the car somewhere else. Somewhere that don't belong to the cigarette man?"

Evans eyed him carefully. In his own way, he had a high regard for Irish Tony, with his singing and his daft jokes. They'd been in many a brawl together, and he knew the fighting quality behind the handsome face. Tony wasn't the man to turn his back on an argument. And yet he didn't fancy taking on King-size Saunders, and there had to be a reason.

"What's wrong with Epping?" he persisted.

Tony shrugged.

"He's mob-handed, that man, for a start. On top of that, we wouldn't be just having a quick punch-up and riding off into the sunset. You know that, Jim, you must do. We'd be starting a bleeding war. Do we really want one?"

When it was put to him like that, Evans could see the point. It was quite true. An expedition to let off steam was one thing. That would do them all good. But a long-running series was another matter, and not one he could reason about properly. It was the sort of thing Charlie would have to decide.

"How about the Elephant, then? There's one or two old mates down there we could call on. That wouldn't start a war. Be more like a bleeding massacre if we get a good start on 'em."

Tony's eyes gleamed. This was more like it. There was one particular villain down there, a greengrocer. Mouthy bastard, he was. Be a pleasure to put him away for a couple of weeks.

"I like the Elephant," he smiled. "Nice glass of beer down there. We'll pop down and have one tonight, eh?''

"Right. Unless Charlie wants us, of course. Where does he get to these days, anyway. Where is he now?''

Tony shrugged. He was wondering the same thing.

Charlie Hurst emptied his mug of coffee and tapped delightedly at the newspaper spread out in front of him. The item was small, only four lines on an inside page, but Charlie regarded it as a sign that all was right with the world. When his first venture as a burglar had received no publicity, his relief had been tinged with anxiety. Like every other criminal, Charlie firmly believed that the entire forces of law and order were organised solely for the purpose of pinning something on him, getting him behind bars. The burglary at George Blandford's house had been hushed up for some reason, and he had a lingering suspicion that, somehow, a connection had been made with himself. Jeremy Newton had tried to persuade him that that was not the case, that the whole thing was too trivial to bother with. But Newton didn't know everything. He certainly didn't know the coppers like Charlie did. Still, the days had gone by, and after a while he felt safer. They didn't hang about, not with burglary jobs. The great thing was to nobble the bloke with the stuff still on him, and there wasn't much chance of that, after a week.

The second burglary had been even easier than the first. The man was separated from his wife, and lived in a posh block of flats at Regents Park. He'd been out with a little darling when Charlie popped in, and it had been a very profitable twenty minutes. Not as good as the first time, but very nice money. Charlie's original seven thousand pounds had become twelve thousand by the close of business the following day, and he had had a very enjoyable few hours after receiving Newton's telephone call.

That had been a fortnight ago. On the previous evening he'd carried out his third job, and he had to hand it to Newton. A bloke had to be right on the inside to come up with all this valuable information. He'd never steered him wrong yet, not even on the smallest detail. Charlie had bought the midday editions without much hope. They hadn't bothered with the first two, so why make an exception out of this one? Nevertheless, he worked his way laboriously through each page, and was finally rewarded by the tiny paragraph on page eight.

LORD NEWNHAM ROBBED

Thieves broke into the Mayfair home of Lord Newnham today, and escaped with £80 worth of small items. 'I was lucky,' said his lordship, 'they missed the silver in the next room.' Police enquiries are proceeding.

Charlie chuckled. Missed the silver indeed. Fine mug he'd have looked, getting his collar felt for a sackful of knives and forks. Some hopes. Still and all, it was in the bleeding papers at last. And no mention of the earlier jobs, so they hadn't put two and two together.

What was the time? He'd slept longer than he meant to. Better get down to the Crown. Those two would be wondering about him.

Twenty minutes later he pushed into the throng of shirt-sleeved men, looking for his henchmen. There they were. Blimey, they had enough booze on the table. Charlie hoped they weren't going it too strong. Booze was a terrible thing if you didn't handle it properly.

Reaching the table, he nodded.

"Christ, it's hot. Can I have one of those?"

Without waiting for an answer he picked up a glass of beer and took a swallow. Then he made a face.

"Warm," he said in disgust.

"It's all the same," shrugged Tony. "All the pubs are suffering. As fast as they get the beer in the punters start swallowing it. It don't have a chance to get cold."

"Bleeding disgrace," grumbled Charlie, pulling out a chair. "Well, what's on then?"

They had been deep in conversation when he arrived, and he was wondering what had engaged them so closely.

"Nothing special," Tony hedged.

Charlie looked at him sharply. He hoped he wasn't going to have any trouble with these two. At odd moments, during the past few weeks, he'd caught each of them looking at him in a rather questioning way. Could be his imagination, could be the heat. But Charlie Hurst always liked to know exactly where he stood.

"It didn't look like nothing when I came in," he said pointedly. "You looked to me like two blokes with something on their minds."

They both stared at the table. He was convinced now that something was up. It wasn't possible, was it, that they'd cottoned on to Mr. Patrick Owen? He remembered the time he'd bumped into Johnny Barker outside Harrods. Cunning sod, that Johnny. If he'd followed him that day— But how could he? All that nonsense with the two taxis and everything. No. No, it wasn't Johnny Barker. Still, he must know what it was.

"Well," he tapped at the table sharply, "what's coming off?"

It was Mad Jimmy who finally answered him.

"Not a lot, Charlie. We're feeling the heat, that's all. Getting a bit restless."

Irish Tony joined in.

"We need some exercise, Charlie. Got to keep in practice, haven't we?"

He looked at each in turn with narrowed eyes. If these two comics thought he was going for King-size Saunders, they were in for some nasties.

"What d'you mean, exercise," he asked softly.

"Bit of excitement, Charlie, that's all." Tony tried to sound reassuring.

"Down the Elephant way," added Evans. "They've been getting a bit saucy these days. Thought we'd pay a little social call. If it's all right with you, Charlie, that is."

Charlie thought about it. King-size Saunders had no connection with the Elephant. If that was all these two were cooking up, it might not be a bad move. It wasn't good for people to get too stale in their way of business.

And it was certainly nothing to do with Mr. Patrick Owen.

The more he thought about the idea, the better he liked it. Good. Yes, it was good. His face split into a grin, and he slapped the table.

"Why not? Why not? A little outing will do us all good."

The other two exchanged glances.

"Us?" queried Tony. "You mean you're coming with us?"

Charlie patted him on the shoulder.

"Coming with you, my son? Of course I'm coming. Some nasty men down that way. Nasty rough men. Can't have you going down there without me to look after you. Yes, we'll do that. Have to be late on, though. Not before nine o'clock."

"That's all right, Charlie," enthused Evans. "Won't be much going on before half ten anyway. I'm looking forward to this."

"Bit of healthy exercise, as my old vicar used to say. One thing though, lads," Charlie's voice became serious, "lay off this stuff tonight. You can have all you want, afterwards. Swim in it, if you like. Afterwards. You got me?"

The others nodded, in pleasurable anticipation.

Charlie was satisfied. By the time they went he would have had his telephone call from Jeremy Newton.

That ought to be something to celebrate.

EIGHT

Mara Newton stood in front of the full-length mirror, examining her body critically. She was entirely naked, and her concern at that moment was that her suntan should be even all over. Most women spoiled the effect of a good tan by tell-tale white patches here and there, where the dictates of modesty demanded a certain minimal coverage. That was Mara's opinion, and to correct the deficiency she had contrived a sheltered sun-bathing spot on the roof of the house. Here she had no need of those bothersome scraps of material which kept the sun from doing its work properly. The roof was quite safe, except for the occasional sortie by helicopters from the squadron stationed a few miles away, and if one of those appeared on the scene she merely rolled over on to her stomach and waited until it had passed. Not that she really cared anyway, but she didn't want her photograph appearing on the walls of squadron huts.

Satisfied with her inspection, she patted gently at her flank and smiled. Someone was due for a delightful surprise, and she wondered fleetingly who it might be.

Since that awful scene when she had given Tom Gardner his marching orders Mara had not yet found a suitable successor. Not that there was any lack of candidates. That had never been a problem for her since she had been sixteen years old, but she had become very selective in these last few years. A man had to appeal to her on several levels before she would consider embarking on a liaison. She was, after all, quite a catch, and had no desire to be regarded as what the hunters called 'easy meat'. It was a disgusting expression, but she could see the justice of it, and indeed it could well be applied to several of the bored housewives in her own circle of acquaintances. She had no intention of joining them, and the need was not there, nor would it be for another ten years. Turning to one side, she arched her back, and purred with self-satisfaction. Make that fifteen years, she decided.

Next, she wondered vaguely what to wear at the Latham's that evening, but it was too early to worry about that yet. Leave it until Jeremy comes home, she decided, perhaps he might have some thoughts about it. If he could be persuaded to take any interest, that was. Jeremy was up to something, she had no doubt about that, and she was becoming increasingly concerned as to what it might be. He was preoccupied rather more often than was his custom, and there was the odd unexplained evening in town. It might never have dawned on her to notice, if she hadn't mislaid that letter from her mother, weeks before. It contained the new address of one of her aunts, and she wanted it to insert in the address book.

After searching everywhere she could think of, she had asked him about it.

"You haven't got mother's letter, have you, darling?"

Jeremy looked up from his paper.

"Letter? No. Why should I have it?"

"It's just that I can't find it anywhere."

He grunted.

"Better go through your forty-seven handbags."

She stuck out her tongue. Her handbags were a standing source of irritation between them. There was a time when she had got a bit out of hand, she admitted. Jeremy had inspected her latest acquisition and accused her of having 'about a hundred' already. She had reacted by demanding that they count them together. The actual number was fourteen, and it certainly was excessive. But it wasn't a hundred. Since then, Jeremy always quoted the first number that came into his head. Last time it had been thirty-five. Today it was forty-seven. The market was definitely rising, and next time he did it she would insist on another count.

But not now. The letter was the important thing. Her husband had buried his face in the newspaper again.

"You had it this morning."

"Eh?"

"The letter. You had it this morning."

Mildly annoyed, he raised his eyes again.

"Had what? Are you still on about that letter?"

"Yes. Don't you remember, I gave it to you, and you

said you'd read it.''

"Of course I remember. And I did read it. Gave it back to you."

Mara shook her head.

"No you didn't. I was clearing the table."

"Then I must have put it down somewhere. It can't be far. This isn't all that big a house. It'll turn up."

But it didn't. The only place Mara hadn't looked was in his study. There wasn't exactly a rule about it, but it was tacitly understood between them that she did not go into that room unless there was a particular reason. In their early days she had made a couple of well-meaning attempts to straighten up his desk, and the resultant exchange between them still lingered in the memory.

She'd have to look, though. The letter could be anywhere, among all that rubbish. After Jeremy had driven off the next day, she went into his study, feeling that quite unnecessary twinge of guilt as she entered. The letter was not to be found, but she made a discovery that unnerved her. The centre drawer of the desk was locked. Jeremy had never locked it before. In fact, Mara had never really known whether he even owned a key for it. But he obviously did, and he'd started to use it.

Why?

The only person even remotely likely to go near the desk was herself.

It followed, therefore, that whatever was locked away was something she was not supposed to see. Immediately her mind turned to her own activities, and in particular to Tom Gardner. The affair was cooling off then, but it had been quite hectic for several months. Perhaps Jeremy was on to it. Perhaps he'd hired someone, one of those nasty private enquiry people, to keep an eye on her. People like that made reports, didn't they? A thing of that sort would certainly need to be locked up. It didn't have to be that, of course. It could be something else. Yes, but what, for example? Rack her brains as she might Mara could not come up with an alternative which was remotely convincing.

Giving one last futile tug at the drawer, she went off in search of a key that might open it. She tried every small key she could lay her hands on, but it was no use. The desk was very old, with ornate brasswork handles, and no doubt the key would be one of those intricate little affairs. Mara spent much of that day in feverish speculation, and even cancelled a hair appointment.

When her husband finally arrived home she insisted on drawing his bath herself, which pleased him, but excited no suspicion. Why should it? The moment he was safely out of the way she searched through his pockets. In addition to the ring with his car keys on it, she found a smaller one with two keys, one of which could well be the right one, judging by the ornate metalwork.

Mara rushed downstairs to the study, feeling quiet triumph as the key turned smoothly and the drawer finally lay open before her. There were papers inside, and these she drew out with trembling fingers. Nothing but figures. Boring old figures. Why should Jeremy bother to lock this stuff out of sight? There were a couple of letters in there, from a firm of stockbrokers, whose name even she knew, but why hide them? She pulled the drawer free of the desk to satisfy herself that the fatal report on herself wasn't tucked away at the far end. Nothing. What on earth was going on? Frowning now, she read the letters. Well, it certainly seemed that Jeremy was doing very well at the moment. But then, as she freely admitted, the workings of finance were a great mystery to her. Jeremy had often tried to explain the way money went up and down, and that much of it was meaningless in real terms. Still, according to these letters it was very much an 'up' situation at the moment. Funny that, because just the other evening he'd been complaining that they had better not have a new car this year.

So far as Mara could tell, Jeremy seemed to be the joint beneficiary—was that the word, or did that only apply to wills?—anyway, he seemed to be in cahoots with one P. Owen Esq.

Owen. She'd heard that name before. Yes, of course. That was the name of Jeremy's gangster, the one who'd come to the house a few weeks earlier. Patrick Owen, that was the man. Oh, all right, Jeremy said he wasn't a gangster at all, and perhaps he wasn't, technically. But he had a lot of money he didn't want to account for, and Mara knew that didn't happen to people who worked from nine to five. Unexplained cash meant gambling, or something the police didn't approve of. Yes, she remembered him quite clearly now, remembered the unspoken challenge in his eyes.

A roar from upstairs proclaimed an absence of towels. Mara replaced the papers carefully, locked the drawer, and went back to the bedroom. Something was going on, and now that she knew about it her relief at learning that it didn't concern herself and Tom Gardner was overtaken by her curiosity. What were they up to, this man Owen and Jeremy? And why shouldn't she know about it?

That had been some time ago, and since then she had opened the drawer at regular intervals. There were more papers now, and, if her limited understanding of their import was the correct one, the firm of Patrick Owen and Jeremy Newton was doing very nicely, thank you. But, of course, she could be wrong. And, in any case, none of that would explain why Jeremy would suddenly become so preoccupied at times. Nor would it account for these evenings in London. Stockbrokers don't work at night. In her lighter moments she devised some strange activities for these two unlikely associates. They were running a string of high-class brothels, that was one solution. Jeremy would put up the capital and the brains. Owen would supply the necessary muscle. She could recall the ripple of those muscles with pleasure. Or, they were running some kind of system at the gaming tables which was paying handsome dividends.

She tried to raise the question of Owen on one occasion.

"Guess who I thought I saw in London today?"

They were having a salad that evening, because of the heat, and also because she wouldn't have had time to prepare anything more involved. Jeremy hated salad. He munched morosely at a piece of lettuce.

"No idea. Who?"

"Your gangster friend. The one with the silver Mercedes. What was his name?"

He frowned in irritation.

"Told you before, he's not a gangster. Did you ever hear of the law of slander?"

Mara pouted.

"Don't be so stuffy. We haven't had salad for weeks. Anyway, you haven't told me his name."

"His name is Owen," he told her shortly.

"Ah yes. Thought I saw him in Bond Street."

"Oh?"

If Jeremy was interested, he concealed the fact very well. Blast the man. She persisted.

"Well, it certainly looked like him. Could it have been?"

Jeremy heaved his shoulders, and wished she'd talk about something else.

"Could have been, I suppose. You were in London. He lives in London. Could have been."

"Yes, but Bond Street," she frowned. "He's not exactly Bond Street, would you say?"

Jeremy wagged a finger.

"That's a typical suburban remark. You always refer to him as a gangster. Half of Bond Street is entirely devoted to whores and poodles. Who do you imagine they work for? Belted earls?"

"No need to be crude," she sniffed. "Anyway, I wasn't sure. Do you think it could have been him, then?

Does he live near there?"

With evident reluctance Jeremy lowered his paper. This was going to need handling with some care, he realised. Perhaps Mara was just making conversation, and then again, perhaps she wasn't. Some of her most innocent-seeming remarks were the result of deep thought, not to say devious thought, as she spun some finely laced piece of intrigue together. The subject of Patrick Owen was not one on which he cared to elaborate in the slightest. Time enough when the news of their successful partnership began to permeate the financial world. Even then, they would be city news, not social news. And at this early stage in the game Jeremy didn't want his silent partner to be any kind of news at all. Why the devil had Mara chosen Bond Street on that particular day? Why couldn't she stick to Knightsbridge?

"I don't know his exact address," he said heavily. "I believe he has a place in the West End somewhere, but it's no concern of mine. Our contact is through various city offices. You could always look in the telephone directory if you're that curious about the man."

Mara pouted, playing for time. Surely Jeremy couldn't know she'd already searched the directory, had even taken the trouble to eliminate possible candidates? Their Mr. Owen was not listed, and that added piquancy to her search.

"I'm only making conversation, darling. Trying to get you to tear your attention away from that boring old paper for five minutes. We needn't talk about him if you'd rather not. Let's talk about something else."

She was dangerous now, and her husband knew all the signs.

"I'm not trying to avoid the subject of Mr. Owen, dear. It's just that I don't know much about the man, and I've.had very little to do with him."

He sounded reasonable, almost conciliatory. Mara was thankful she was not a field creature, not a rabbit or a squirrel, because if she had been her nose would be twitching nineteen to the dozen. There he sat, her reasonable husband, with a wide smile on his face. Lying his head off. Lying to her quite deliberately and easily. But why? That was the point. He and this Owen were up to their ears in some scheme or other. There was too much continuous correspondence in the locked drawer for it to be otherwise. Yet here he was, denying anything much more than a passing acquaintance with the man.

It was disconcerting, to put it mildly. In fact, it was much worse than that. Jeremy had always been so open and frank with her about everything that it never occurred to her to doubt anything he said. Looking at him now, listening to him, she knew that under other circumstances she would be totally deceived. It was only because she knew perfectly well that he wasn't telling the truth that she was able to resist him. And, if that was the case in this instance, how many other times had there been in the past when he had displayed the same disarming frankness? How many other times had he been lying, just as he was now?

She dismissed the whole thing.

"Well, let's forget him, shall we?"

Jeremy struggled hard to keep relief from his face and his tone.

"As you wish. By the way, did Lettie Hughes say anything about this confounded croquet do of hers on Saturday?"

So the subject of Patrick Owen was shunted to one side. For his part, Jeremy was highly relieved that Mara had decided not to push the matter, out of sheer caprice. From the way she was babbling on now it was evident that the question of her partner on the coming Saturday was a matter of far more serious import.

Mara prattled away, using only the top half of her mind. In her deeper thoughts she now knew positively that Jeremy was up to something. Something serious, something that mattered enough for him to keep it from her, even to the extent of locking his desk and telling her outright lies. It would have to be very important for him to go to those lengths. Important enough, therefore, for her to treat with extreme caution. No more frontal attacks, like the abortive attempt just concluded. She'd watch the mail more closely, listen to his telephone calls, and above all, keep monitoring the desk drawer. All this was stirring in the back of her head as she twittered on.

"—and if I find myself stuck with that awful Major Brawby, I'll have one of my sick headaches on the spot. Oh, you can laugh, Jeremy. But I'm perfectly serious. That man *paws*."

So it had passed off. Jeremy was quietly satisfied that the subject of Mr. Patrick Owen was closed as a result of their conversation that evening. Since then, Mara had instituted a system of checking on him, being careful to remain unobtrusive. It would never do for him to suspect for a moment what she was up to. Time enough for that when she had fathomed the game. The problem· was, she was really no further forward than when she started. Except for the growing correspondence in the desk drawer, Mara had been unable to find anything untoward in Jeremy's affairs, so far as she had access to them. But there was no doubt, since she had been on the look-out for signs, that there was something on his mind. She had come to associate the whole mystery with his recent habit of going back to London in the evenings, or sometimes delaying his return home by several hours. Under other circumstances she would have suspected there was a woman in the background, and she would have known exactly how the deal with that little problem. As a precautionary check, and to eliminate the other woman theory for good, she had put Jeremy to the test on two occasions on his return from London. She recalled both evenings with pleasure and satisfaction. Jeremy's activities with her had demonstrated quite clearly that he had not been sleeping with anyone else in the course of the evening. Even his considerable stamina had its limits.

Today he had been down on business to some firm of solicitors in Kent. On his return there would be a couple of hours to spare before they had to leave for the Lathams. The vexed question of her dress would need to be settled.

Outside, she heard Jeremy's car pulling into the

drive.

He had not enjoyed the day. It had started well enough, with his early morning dash to the photography club, where he had collected the now-familiar envelope slipped through the letter-box by Charlie Hurst. Having obtained the information he needed, he telephoned his stockbroker and gave certain instructions. All that remained then was to await the inevitable jump in the value of his new holdings. It had come as an unwelcome surprise to be told that he'd have to go down into Kent.

"What?"

The vehemence of his reply when he heard the news was not the usual way he spoke to Peggy, his secretary.

"I'm sorry, Mr. Newton, but I'm only passing on a message."

He pulled himself together at once.

"Didn't mean to jump, Peggy. Bit of a surprise, that's all. I'd made a number of arrangements for today, assuming Mr. Halton would deal with that Kent business. Still, if he's stuck in Glasgow that's all there is to it."

Instead of being able to keep an eye on what was happening in the city, Jeremy had been compelled to make the trip. It was an annual chore, and no one really wanted to go, but the county firm put a lot of business their way in the course of a twelvemonth. Jeremy put the best face on it that he could, and was able to get away by mid-afternoon, when he went straight home.

Now he saw Mara, standing, or perhaps posing

would be a better word, at the foot of the stairs and looking radiant.

"You're back early," she greeted brightly. "We can have a quiet laze around before we have to go out."

The Lathams, of course. It seemed as if the whole damned world was conspiring against him today. He shook his head regretfully.

"Fraid not, love. I only popped in for a quick cup of tea. I'll have to go back to the office tonight, get my report in about today's trip."

"Oh dear." Mara made a face. "Well, we're due at eight, you know."

"Eight for eight-thirty, surely? Well, I hope to God it is. There's no way I can be back here for eight. Look, will you telephone them, and explain that I'm in a fix? I'll run all the way there and back, I promise."

Mara made a gesture of impatience.

"It's too bad of you. I wanted you to help me pick out something to wear."

"Wear?" He wasn't really paying attention. "Well, what about that mauve thing? You look like Miss World in that."

"For God's sake, Jeremy, at least try. That mauve thing, as you call it, is solid wool from head to foot. It's eighty in the shade today. Perhaps I should wear my fur coat and wellingtons with it?"

He really hadn't time to waste on this sort of nonsense. He had to get the market closing situation report, and he had to make his own report to Mr. Patrick Owen. Not that he could explain any of that to this angry woman in front of him.

"Tell you what, I won't waste time with tea. I'll get straight off," he decided. "Give me a better chance of not being late."

"Don't you dare be late," she threatened.

"I'm off then."

Out he went to the car, and was quickly gone.

Mara stood in the doorway, her mind very busy. Then she picked up her handbag from the hall table, extracted her car keys, and went out to the garage.

NINE

It seemed as though the long, golden summer would never end. July came and went, August had been the hottest month for thirty years, fifty years or within living memory, according to which newspaper the reader happened to be holding at the time. Records were being smashed daily. The most hours of sunshine, the highest temperature, the lowest water-levels, so it went on. Even now, in early September, the home beaches were doing record business, and there was no sign of any break in the weather, according to the long-term forecasters.

The British people, with that adaptability for which they were noted, had welcomed their new rôle as quasi-Mediterraneans with open arms. Light-weight clothing, dark glasses and even peasant straw hats were the order of the day. A visitor to the metropolis might have been forgiven for the assumption that he had disembarked at Honolulu by mistake. The pace of life itself had slowed, and the spirit of mañana was manifest. Nobody hurried any more, and accepted that no one else was going to hurry either.

For the criminal fraternity it was Christmas every day. In the absence of jackets and heavy handbags, the pickpockets were only restricted in the amount they could steal by the volume they could carry. With every window in the country flung wide in search of an elusive breath of fresh air, the breaking and entering brigade had a heyday. There was gambling fever, too. People would bet on any event, so long as the physical exertion was to be undertaken by others. Horses, athletes, sportsmen of all kinds, it was all one to the punters. Absenteeism rose sharply, and puzzled managers found a whole new vein of reasons in the sickness certificates. Heat rash, dehydration, exhaustion, all faithfully signed by the overworked general practitioners.

As always, the people who were prepared to put themselves out in the new conditions were making a very comfortable thing of it all. Suppliers of refreshment, entertainment, every form of relaxation, were raking in money hand over fist.

The relentless, continuing sun left no one unaffected. That included Charlie Hurst.

The notification of Rathbone-Hurst, C., of his intention to be known in future as Patrick Owen had attracted no attention whatever. Charlie's gamble had succeeded, and Owen now existed legally. He was a wealthy man, the new Mr. Owen, with a sum not far short of six figures to his credit. Charlie liked everything about his coming new existence, and would spend an increasing amount of time at Parkside South, thinking himself into the new life. Wearing the clothes, including the hot climate garb he had acquired from the most famous tropical outfitters in London. Reading, too, occupied a lot of his time. Charlie's reading had been confined to the back pages for years, but now he wanted to know more about the kind of existence he could look forward to, after he said goodbye to Charlie Hurst forever. He ·had been accustomed to having a great deal of money to spend for many years past, but long before he had met Jeremy Newton, Charlie had become aware of the futility of spending money, beyond a certain point. He had found himself once, a couple of years earlier, suddenly trying to put his feelings into words. The result had not been rewarding.

It was a simple enough occasion that started him off. Some builder's labourer up North had won half a million pounds on the football pools.

"Look at this, eh, Charlie? Half a million nicker. Stone me, eh? Stone me. Lucky bleeder."

It had been Irish Tony who raised it. Charlie took him up.

"What would you do, if it was you, Tony?"

His handsome companion started.

"Do?" he repeated. "I'd get out of here for a start. Spain, that's me. You can't go wrong in Spain. Half a dozen litres, and a dozen señoritas, eh, Jim?"

"Right," nodded Jimmy Evans. "But you wouldn't leave your old mates behind?"

"Gawd, no," denied Tony. "Come one, come all, that's me. We'd have the biggest bleeding fiesta they've ever seen, I tell you. Cor, just think of it, eh?"

Charlie felt impatience rising within him.

"Well, go on then," he encouraged. "All you've done so far is to spend a few hundred quid on booze, and birds. We're talking about half a million now. What else will you do?"

Tony closed his eyes.

"Biggest hotel, it would be. All me mates, all the birds we can manage. Plus a few spares, for a change like. And grub. Mustn't forget that. Sodding great steaks, a foot thick. Every meal."

"And music," Evans butted in. "I know it's your money, Tony, but you wouldn't mind spending a few bob on some music, eh?"

Tony, in his new-found largesse, raised his arm grandly.

"Christ, no. Have who you like. Straight off Top of the Pops. All expenses paid. Just send the bill to me. I'll be in the bridal suite, with the King of Spain's daughter I shouldn't be surprised."

"You still haven't said a word about what you'll do with the money," insisted Charlie. "All you've said so far is that you're going to fill your belly all day and night, and screw every tart you can lay hands on. What else?"

"What else?"

His two companions looked at each other. They were mystified. Mustn't give Charlie Hurst any offence of course. He could be very funny, Charlie could, if people upset him. But what was he on about?

"How d'you mean, Charlie? What else is there?"

Their leader knew it was hopeless. These people weren't even on his wavelength. But he had one more try.

"Just think about it for a minute," he suggested. "How much steak can one man eat? How much booze can he swallow? How many birds can he screw, really? What I'm saying is, when you've done all that you've still spent hardly anything. What will you do next?"

Tony nodded, trying to understand.

"Yeah, I see what you mean. You mean, after we've really worked 'em over in Spain. Then what happens?"

"Right," nodded Charlie.

Evans chuckled.

"Obvious, innit? When we get sick of it over there we just send out for an airplane—"

"—who sends out for an airplane?" Tony interrupted.

"Sorry, Tony, if it's all right with you, that is. It's your do. We'll have to ask the gent in the bridal suite if it's all right, first."

Tony nodded, mollified. He wasn't having people chucking his money about without asking him.

"Go on, then."

"Why, we pack up and go. Shove a few crates on the plane, kiss the girls goodbye and just go."

"Go where?"

"Italy, of course. Start of all over again. New birds, new scenery, the whole lot."

He was smart, that Jimmy, reflected Tony, grinning.

"There you are then, Charlie. And after that we'll do America."

"Then Hawaii. Lift a few grass skirts."

"Right. Then where? Japan. That's it, Japan."

"Wrong way round in Japan," mused Evans.

They both exploded with laughter. Charlie smiled, and gave it up. They hadn't understood a word he said.

But now he needn't concern himself with people like that any longer. There was more to life than being sick every day in a hundred pounds a night hotel, and Charlie wanted to learn about it.

He read indiscriminately. Social news, furniture articles, house prices, it was all grist to Charlie's mill. Of course, he wasn't yet ready to embark properly on his new existence. There was more money to be made first, but he was beginning to have doubts, even about that. He'd got a lot of money already, and he was no longer certain that he needed the amount agreed on originally. He was the one who took the chances, after all. A bloody fine look-out, if he had to start off his new life spending six months in the nick. It was all right for Newton. It wasn't him, sweating with fear in somebody else's house at two o'clock in the morning. No, Charlie was far from convinced of the need to risk his liberty many more times. A clever man always knew when enough was enough, and Charlie had a feeling that day wasn't far away.

On top of that, he was becoming increasingly resentful when it was time to cease being Patrick Owen, and go back to Charlie Hurst's life. The shoddy furnished flat, the endless steak and chip meals, the sitting around in pubs. All the pleasure was gone out of all that, now.

Perhaps it wouldn't be too long.

For Mara Newton, the summer had not been a success, and there were two major reasons.

First and foremost was the deepening mystery about Jeremy and Patrick Owen. That afternoon, weeks before, when she had decided to follow Jeremy, she had managed to keep him in sight quite successfully, almost to the end. One·white Mini looks like another, and so she wasn't too worried about being spotted on his tail. If he had accused her of it, she had a good story all ready. She suspected he was seeing another woman and wanted to find out for herself. In the event, she had got away with it, but just failed in her objective at the last moment. In the late afternoon crawl at Hyde Park, Jeremy had just got away at a traffic signal which was against her when she reached it. But one thing was certain. He had been heading away from the office, not towards it, and she had no doubt in her own mind that his destination was a rendezvous with the man Owen.

Since then their business affairs had gone from strength to strength, if the desk drawer was to be believed. That was good, and certainly no one had more reason to wish Jeremy success than Mara had. But he never referred to it. Quite the reverse, in fact. He kept on pleading poverty, even over the simple question of a holiday.

"It doesn't have to be anywhere grand," she had protested. "If the worst comes to the worst, we could go on one of these package tours."

Jeremy grimaced.

"Oh lovely. Fish and chips in Majorca, you mean?"

"Now don't be difficult, dear. You know perfectly well I don't mean anything of the kind. No. There are some quite reasonable sounding things on offer."

Her husband sighed.

"Look, you know as well as I do what's involved. If it's cheap, you get saddled with these ghastly vino-in-braces people. If it isn't cheap, if they really are offering something acceptable, the only people you'll find are retired master plumbers from Liverpool. Now let's drop it, there's a dear girl. We can't afford a decent holiday, so why don't we just take the kids to the coast, and leave it at that? Dammit, we're having the finest summer in thirty years."

"Forty," she corrected. "The *Express* said forty."

"All right then, forty. All the more reason to be satisfied with a bucket and spade job."

But she hadn't been satisfied. Not only was she piqued with his uncharacteristic meanness, but she didn't want the claustrophobic restrictions of a seaside hotel. Mara had not been having any luck in finding a successor to Tom Gardner, and she knew she wasn't going to find one in the atmosphere of a family hotel. That was the second major reason for her dissatisfaction.

Finally, Jeremy had given in. Partly. He would not go with her, but he agreed that she and Veronica Tate should go off together, and that was what had happened.

Mara had set out with high hopes on that venture. If

a couple of man-eaters like Veronica and herself couldn't find some suitable companions in a place like Greece, then things weren't what they used to be.

In the event, the trip was a failure. There was a positive dearth of people whom one could possibly associate with. The unattached males were either elderly predators, or young fitters on the loose from Birmingham. How Jeremy would have relished it all, she reflected bitterly on the hot, romantic, manless evenings. Finally, in an excess of boredom, she had given herself to one of the local fishermen. That had been a disaster. The man was unskilled and brutal. On top of that, he smelled of onion soup.

Now, lying on her protected sun roof, she examined the deep rich tan which was spread evenly all over her body. What a waste. Even Jeremy scarcely bothered with her lately. That was partly due to the heat, she knew, but it also owed something to his preoccupation with other matters. Whatever they might be.

A distant buzzing, like a swarm of angry bees, warned her that a helicopter was not far off. The noise grew louder, and she could just see it now in the distance and coming in her direction. It was one of the larger ones, she noted, the ones Jeremy said were used for parachute jumping practice. He said they would normally carry ten or twelve jumpers, in addition to the normal crew members. The roar of the engine signified the increasing closeness of the machine, and this was the usual signal for Mara to reach for her towel, or at the least to turn over and lie on her front.

She thought of the men up there. Fit, vigorous young

men, crouched in the metal hull of the chopper, awaiting the command that would launch them out into the bright blue sky, with a drop of thousands of feet. How exciting it would be to do that, she reflected. To join those lovely muscular young bodies hurtling out into space. Thrilling.

The helicopter was very close now. Time to move.

Mara lay quite still, and stared upwards through the dark glasses.

Jeremy Newton sat at his desk, an unread affidavit in front of him. A man could not be expected to concentrate properly in this stuffy heat. Everybody was suffering of course, it wasn't just him. Every day there were more excuses being made for delays, failures to complete, and so forth. And, only yesterday, old Branston had telephoned all the way from the south of France to enquire whether he could extend his holiday by a further week. Branston, of all people. One of those chaps people set their clocks by, a dry, humourless man, pillar of the community type. Even he was feeling the pull of the lotus, and Lord knew, he was in the right place for it. Lucky sod.

In the dusty stillness of the room Jeremy smiled at the thought. He had never expected to see the day when he would envy old Branston. It was a momentary thing anyway. He had no cause to envy anyone, these days. The scheme was working well, and he was well satisfied with the way they were progressing. Mind you, he pointed out to himself, it had not been a madcap venture from the outset. Ever since the idea had first entered his mind, been rejected, and forced its way back in again, he had known there would be a great deal of thought required before theory could be translated into action. Many was the hour he had spent at this desk, and in his study at home, working out details to the *n*th degree. Carrying out mock exercises, too, against actual events in the City. Honing and eliminating, examining every development in depth. Probing, doubting, accepting nothing at its face value at the altar of self-deception. If ever the scheme was to become reality, he knew there would be no room for error. Even in those initial stages he had begun to cultivate the need for personal caution. Every scrap of paper he used, every scribbled note, was gathered together at the end of the day and ceremoniously destroyed. Jeremy worked with people equally as alert and intelligent as himself. People who would quickly find significance in the idlest of jottings. It was up to him to ensure they didn't get the opportunity.

Then, when he was satisfied that the plan was viable, he had a further major obstacle to overcome, the need to find the right man to carry out the criminal part. When he had told Charlie Hurst he'd spent two years looking for him, it had been an exaggeration, but not a very great one. The time actually devoted to the search was one year and nine months. In all that time he had found only one other man who seemed to meet all his requirements. Then, a matter of days before he made his approach, the man had been killed in a road accident. That had been a setback, and Jeremy had found himself back at square one.

Charlie Hurst was a real find. Intelligent, shrewd and tough, he had all the qualities Jeremy was seeking. On top of that, he was a man one could get on with, and that was very important in a venture of this kind. This plan of Hurst's, to disappear into the character of Patrick Owen, only confirmed the justness of Newton's choice. It was a most sensible solution to the problem of adjustment to his new financial standing, and once he had been taken into Hurst's confidence he had encouraged the idea with enthusiasm.

And now they were at the very brink of success. Two, or at the most three, more moves and the target would have been achieved. A more excitable man might have felt well pleased with life and anxious to move ahead. Jeremy Newton was not an excitable type. He was a man who planned each move with the greatest possible care, and at that moment he was not thinking in the narrow terms of the next step. He was wondering whether it was not now time to suspend activity entirely. The operative word was 'suspend', because he had no intention of abandoning the great outline. They had moved a long way in a few months, and, as is the way of things, people were beginning to sit up. At first, he had been another speculator who was having a run of luck. There were always a few of those around, and they attracted nothing more than the occasional wink, or the knowing nudge. But the 'win a few, lose a few' syndrome would normally come into its own after a while. A dip in the fortunes of Newton and his partner, the silent Mr. Owen, was only to be expected. The one point at issue was when it would occur. If it did not, then attention would become focused rather more sharply as people waited for the next move.

Jeremy was not prepared to plunge. He and Hurst had taken large risks to reach their present stage, and no one knew better than he how quickly those gains could turn to losses. He did not intend to lose money, merely to satisfy other people's expectations. Nevertheless, he did not want to attract undue notice, and was wondering at that moment whether the best course might not be merely to stand still. Do nothing. Remain at the present stage for—what—six months? A year? After all, they were not dealing with a win-or-lose bet on the Derby, with a quick celebration at the other end of it. They were preparing themselves for an entirely new life-style, a permanent state of affairs, and the question of timing, if it involved waiting a few months, was scarcely onerous.

It was annoying, of course. After all this time, and the trouble already taken, it was a pity to have to stand within sight of the winning-post with only a few hurdles left to jump. No, that wouldn't do. The analogy was all wrong, and he mustn't think in those terms. There was no race involved. He wouldn't be standing there watching the other runners going past him, winning, leaving him behind. It wasn't a contest. In a more realistic sense he would merely be freezing the film, the way they did on television sometimes. When he was ready to continue everything would be exactly as it had been before the break. Yes, that was a very much better comparison. He'd have to have a very serious talk with Charlie Hurst about the way he was coming to view things. Charlie was not a hired employee, doing whatever Jeremy directed. He was a full partner, a man of strong views, and with the forceful personality to convey them. Yes, he'd need to have a long discussion with Charlie.

No one else was involved. Not directly, anyway. Mara knew nothing whatever, and he had no intention that she ever should. When it was all over, of course, she would benefit from their change in status, and would probably think she was married to some kind of financial wizard. Let her think it, or anything else she chose. Just so long as she never suspected the truth. She'd probably just look at the money and give a great cheer, he reflected. Mara wasn't the girl to go bothering her head about where it came from. It would be there, and that would be what counted. It would certainly cheer her up a bit, and heaven knew she could do with that. These past months she seemed to have become rather edgy. Fractious, almost. He'd have to take some of the blame for that, he admitted. Although he planned meticulously, and left no possibility of error before he set Charlie in motion, there was always that unknown factor, that tiny break in the chain that could put them both in the dock. He'd always been aware of it, and weighed it with utmost care in all his calculations, eliminating it to the fullest extent of which he was capable. But it was always there, and he knew it. What he had not been able to foresee was the strain even that tiny element could put on a man. The hours of wondering, suppose this had happened, what if that had gone wrong, fruitless, unanswerable questions, but a strain none the less.

Yes, there was no doubt that he would have to shoulder some of the responsibility for Mara's present frame of mind. She would have sensed the change in him, the way women do, and it would be up to him to restore the position as quickly as he could. If Hurst and he decided to call a temporary halt then the strain would be taken away, and he could put more of himself into that relationship, as in the past.

Ah, but could he? Could he really do that now?

Because, on top of everything else, there was the Veronica Tate situation.

Even now Jeremy wasn't quite sure how that had come about. He didn't think it was due to any forward planning on his part, or on hers for that matter.

It just sort of happened.

The whole thing had started with one of those chance meetings. The kind that could happen to anyone. The two women had only just returned from their holiday in Greece, glowing with deep tans and good health. He had been on his way out for a glass of beer and a sandwich one lunch-time, and suddenly, there she was.

"Jeremy? Good Lord, this town is getting smaller."

He had been surprised to see her, but delighted. Men were always delighted to see Veronica.

A tall, slender woman, with an almost boyish figure, she kept her shining blonde hair carefully tousled around a high cheek-boned face. There was a gentle, dreamlike quality about her deep green eyes which could flash with sudden devil-may-care if something

amused or attracted her. Her clothes were the despair
of every other woman, not because of the money she
spent, or the famous labels. Plenty of people could
duplicate those. Basically, it was because Veronica
was inside them.

"I swear, if Vee decided to turn out in potato sacks
everyone would ask her where she got them."

This, and variations on it, was typical of the reaction
she provoked. Among the women, that was. Among
the men, the reaction was universal and predictable.
To do her justice, Veronica never seemed to overstep
the mark. Occasionally, a man would make a fool of
himself, going too far in his attentions at someone's
dinner-party, but it would be his own fault, not hers.
Women did not dislike her. She was always friendly,
and easy with them, and always quite unaffected.
There was nothing to which they could take exception.
It was only a matter of simple prudence to keep their
husbands on short reins and ensure they were locked
up for the night when Veronica Tate was in the
vicinity.

And now, here she was, in Jeremy Newton's vicinity.

What a piece of luck.

Jeremy beamed with pleasure.

"Hallo, Veronica, you're the last person I expected
to see. Been buying up the whole town?"

She wore no make-up, and the generous lips were a
dark red against white teeth.

"It certainly feels like it," she smiled. "Now then,
what do you big City gents do with starving girls at
lunch-time?"

"Hungry are you? Well, we'll soon fix that. Give me some of those parcels. Now, what sort of lunch does the lady require?"

His mind was ticking off places that might be suitable. Places where none of his crowd could possibly be. Jeremy had no intention of sharing Veronica with any of those sharks.

She pursed her lips thoughtfully.

"Let me see. Nothing too heavy, in this heat. Could the gentleman provide an olive, very large, very green, entirely surrounded by gin?"

He most certainly could.

"Absolutely," he confirmed. "I know a place where the olives are flown in daily, and hand-selected by the proprietor. We'll go there."

"Thank the Lord you turned up. I think I rather overdid the shopping."

"Never mind. No problem now. I can see you to your train when you're ready to leave."

He began to search the traffic for a taxi. Veronica smiled to herself. Jeremy Newton had always been on the list of men for whom she had half an eye. Not that he'd ever suspected it. none of them ever did. She was far too experienced an operator ever to let one man think he might have an advantage over the man next to him. This one had been on her mental list, though, for some time past. It was odd how the list was sometimes affected by chance circumstances.

In this case it was Mara who had moved Jeremy's name several places upwards. They'd been sitting at a small beach café late one night, and Mara had had one extra glass of ouzo. That was when she had suddenly begun to talk about all the money Jeremy was making, and how he thought she knew nothing about it. The man was on his way to becoming some kind of tycoon, along with his mysterious gangster friend. Veronica liked the sound of the gangster type, and was most intrigued by the whole story, making a mental note to look a little further into things when they returned home. She could make no move in their own locality, naturally. She never did. But a girl could scarcely be blamed for bumping into a man in London, in broad daylight. Now could she? She kept the flat going, for just such encounters.

As for Mara, she really didn't feel any qualms in that direction. Anyone who behaved as she had with that hulking brute of a fisherman really had no right to recriminate.

With such a good-looking husband, too.

She said, offhandedly, "Oh, I'm not going back this afternoon. We're having dinner up here tonight. There's a friend of mine who's away in Scotland at the moment. She lets me use her flat to change in on these occasions. It's over in Bayswater. Perhaps if you wouldn't mind just helping me with this stuff as far as that?"

And that was how it had started.

Jeremy knew he was being anything but wise, and the sensible thing to do was to call a halt to the affair.

That was the sensible thing to do, and he realised it perfectly well.

He looked at his watch, and clucked with

impatience. How the time seemed to drag in this weather. It was only two forty-five.

Veronica wouldn't be at Bayswater until four o'clock.

TEN

Charlie Hurst sat down impatiently. Every window in the flat at Parkside South had been flung wide, but even so, the atmosphere was thick and sultry. He wore no clothes at all, and had only recently emerged from the shower, but nothing seemed to help. One good thing about these late September evenings, at least the sun was going down earlier as each day passed. It would still be one or two in the morning before most people could get to sleep. Jeremy Newton was not due until seven-thirty, and there was more than an hour to wait.

It wasn't an interview he was looking forward to at all. Perhaps if he went over everything once again in his mind it would help to pass the time, and also ensure he didn't forget anything when the argument started.

Because there would have to be an argument. Charlie could see no way of avoiding one.

From the beginning he'd always agreed to let Newton set the pace. He would be the one who decided on the next step, when and where it should happen. Charlie had been content to be directed, because the other man was the one with the information, and that counted for a great deal. It had worked well, too. Newton's briefing was always good. Things happened as he said they would, and even the factor of chance hadn't let them down. Not yet, anyway. Charlie had never had any intention of being caught, simply because somebody turned up at the wrong time. A security guard, an unexpected caller, anybody who disturbed Charlie was going to wind up in the hospital, out of harm's way. The two men had never discussed the possibility, not in explicit terms, but Charlie thought he had the measure of his partner by now. Jeremy Newton wasn't the kind of man to burst into tears if some busybody got himself bashed on the head, not if it ensured their safety.

If the geezer happened to die, of course, that might be different. Charlie had seen rougher customers than Newton turn pale at the thought of murder. Faced with the need for the actual extinction of a human life, even some of the most savage people would back off. Charlie Hurst knew that he was not one of them. If it was a question of shutting somebody up, as opposed to his freedom, and the upsetting of this entire apple-cart, Charlie knew what he would do. Had always known, right from the start, and as his fortunes grew, as he had increasingly more to lose, the harder his attitude had become. Charlie's private fortune was in the six-figure bracket now, and he wasn't going to languish in any jail, not for anybody.

Since the last job, Charlie had grown more and more bored with himself, with Charlie Hurst. The life this new bloke would lead, this Owen, that was the life for Charlie. Or Patrick, rather. The house in the country, like Jeremy's place, only better. The winter cruise lark, and all that, that was the style. Patrick Owen's style. The high-class birds, with the posh voices and the morals of alley-cats.

He wanted to get on with it, and that was why he'd asked Jeremy to come and see him. Charlie had always been a cautious man, he wouldn't have achieved his position in the world otherwise, and one of the things he'd fancied about this arrangement was the way Jeremy insisted on keeping it cool. The man had been right, too. Charlie now owned more money than any villain ever came by, except in his dreams. The beauty of it was, all the money was straight. None of your payroll cash, hidden in some outhouse in a dirty sack. Clean, legal money, all accounted for. Only it wasn't quite enough yet. Not quite enough for the new life, for Mr. Patrick Owen. That would come, and there was no way he could think of anybody preventing it.

The thing was, when?

Because, there was no doubt about it, Charlie Hurst was no longer the man he had been. A man did slow down, of course, in that violent world he inhabited. The natural excitement, the frequent, and often totally unjustified, outbreaks of mayhem, came automatically to a bloke in his twenties. These were the signs, the ritual events, which put the mark on him as a man to watch out for. Ten years, fifteen in Charlie's case, brought a mellower attitude. Rough and ruthless as ever, he would find himself weighing up the pros and cons before going into action. It made him no less dangerous, no less respected, but he was a different man from ten years ago, and he knew it. One of these days, in two years, five years, some young lunatic would topple him, put him away. This was the normal sequence of events, and there wouldn't be much he could do about it.

That was all changed now. Charlie Hurst had the chance to get out, and he wanted it. What with the heat, and his own preoccupation with private matters, his own squad had been getting very itchy in the feet. He had been able to control them, this far, but it was only a matter of time before things got out of hand. He couldn't expect them to understand, and it would be fatal to his plans even to try. But they were beginning to wonder about him. Charlie was no longer prepared to sail into somebody over some half-imagined insult, or for a few hundred quid profit. He wasn't bothered enough. A man with a six-figure bank balance doesn't readily put himself at risk of being knifed over a trifle, nor of getting himself a dose of porridge. That man stood to lose too much. The thing for that man to do was to get himself out of it all, and the sooner the better.

Where the hell was that Jeremy?

Jeremy Newton had mixed feelings about the coming session with Charlie Hurst. On the one hand, he was glad of the opportunity to talk with the man. There was important business to be discussed, and it would require careful handling. Jeremy had decided that activity must be suspended for a while, perhaps even as long as a year. For him, after the years he had already spent in planning and waiting, it would be no more than a delay. The point at issue was, would Charlie Hurst be able to adopt quite so phlegmatic a view? Charlie was not the man to relish inactivity. He was a doer, a let's-get-on-with-it type. Not a fool, of course, not rashly impatient, but a man of action for all that. It was not going to be easy, particularly when everything was going so well, to convince Charlie to sit on his haunches for any length of time.

That was on the one hand.

On the other hand was the fact that the meeting had been called by Charlie. Why? It would have to be something important, for him to take such a step. Had something gone wrong? Had somebody spotted him on one of his expeditions, perhaps? Had the police got onto him, somehow? No, that couldn't be. If the police had got wind of what was going on they'd have been to see him, Jeremy, before this. They wouldn't have just sat back in order to give Charlie comfortable time to make arrangements with his partner. They would have pounced. Yes, of course they would. When they moved, they moved quickly.

What, then?

The events of the past few months had begun to affect Jeremy's business life, a development he had not expected to occur quite so early. The City of London is a narrow, almost claustrophobic world of its own, and with set rules and patterns. Nowhere is this more true than in the money markets. It is possible for a man to keep the darkest imaginable secrets, but on a personal level only. A well-known figure could well be running two domestic establishments, or plotting to overthrow the government, or be pursuing the most bizarre sexual outlets, and no one need be any the wiser. But when it comes to matters of money, the picture is very different. Money is the life-force, the very fount of existence, the purpose, it would seem, of life itself.

The emergence of Jeremy Newton as a shrewd and successful speculator was hardly something to pass unnoticed. He had been very careful, not to say ultra-cautious, with every move. The firm of brokers with whom he dealt with was an institution of the highest probity, where the slightest hint of gossip was a matter for instant dismissal. How do people get to know things, then? That is a mystery almost as old as the City itself. But the signs are not to be missed. The extra alertness of the uniformed messengers, the friendly nods from comparative strangers, the unexpected drink at lunch-time, from the 'gentleman at the end of the bar, sir'.

Jeremy's status had never been in question. Junior partner in a well-respected firm, a coming man in his line, undoubtedly, and with the various awards of insignia of progressive rank laid out for collection along the dusty time-corridors ahead.

He suddenly found that corridors could be circum-vented.

"Newton, isn't it?"

Jeremy was startled to realise that the man beside him at the bar, a leading silk, was addressing him.

"Yes. Good morning, Sir Alan."

"Someone was saying you're quite a fisherman. Trout-man, they said."

Jeremy's fishing expeditions had been few, and inglorious, but one does not argue with Queen's Counsel.

"Wouldn't put my claims too high, sir," he replied, with truth.

"Dark horse, eh? Well, I've got a bit of water which should be coming into its own in a few weeks' time. Perhaps you'd like to pop down, eh? Show us how it's done?"

"Delighted, sir. To come, that is. Rather more of a student though, I think."

Sir Alan's eyes twinkled. He had held the record bag for the past three seasons, as everyone knew.

"Well, we'll see. I'll give you a ring, eh?"

Two days later, he had received a printed invitation to lunch with the Eel and Pie Pedlars, one of the most exclusive luncheon clubs in the City.

People were bumping into him rather too often for coincidence.

"Ah, Jeremy, what a bit of luck. I was only saying this morning, wonder what your views are about this Allied-International merger?"

It was all heady stuff, most exhilarating, and Jeremy enjoyed every minute of it. But in the quiet of his own office he was able to view these developments with detachment. It was all very well, on the one hand, to be singled out as a man to watch. The inevitable corollary of that was, that people were watching. And waiting. Not with any sinister motives, but out of plain greed.

They wanted to know what he was going to do next, and when they knew they would follow him. In droves. He agonised about his new position for hours at a stretch, even to the extent of wondering whether it would not pay him to make a couple of unlucky guesses on the market. That should shut people up. But it was too risky, he decided. They might decide that anyone could make a mistake, and that he would be bound to come good again. If that happened he would be several thousand pounds out of pocket, and with the problem unresolved.

It really was a hell of a situation to be in. And now there was this meeting with Charlie Hurst to be got through. A hell of an anticlimax, after the afternoon with Veronica.

Reluctantly, he walked into the entrance hall of Parkside South.

Mara felt nervous, and no wonder. In her world the very mention of private enquiry agents was a matter for raised eyebrows. Nasty little men, in dirty raincoats, taking flashlight photographs through bedroom windows at two o'clock in the morning.

To find oneself under the scrutiny of one of these creatures was an ongoing nightmare for someone like Mara, who could well have been the object of their attentions a dozen times at least over the years. That was not her present problem. Tired of the endless speculation about Jeremy and Owen, she had 'finally come to the conclusion that the only way to get at the truth was to hire a professional. It sounded all very simple, on the face of it. One simply turned to the yellow pages, picked out a name, and made an appointment. But then one paused. How was she to know whether the man of her choice would be reliable? Or trustworthy? One read terrible things in the newspapers about the way some of these people used whatever information they gained for the purposes of blackmail. It wasn't something you could discuss with a friend, either.

"I've found the most marvellous doctor. So sympathetic—" or

"If ever you need a lawyer you must go to this man. My dear, those eyes—"

It wasn't the same kind of thing at all. You couldn't say, "There's this amazing little man, so unobtrusive and creepy, you'd never know he was there—"

No. There was no question of being able to confide in anyone. It was something she would have to do quite alone, and pray that she got the right man.

Mr. Redman had been aptly named, she decided. A square, chunky man, with terrifying beetled eyebrows set well back in red, puffy cheeks. The mottled texture of his skin, particularly around the nose, was a clear indication that Mr. Redman conducted a lot of his enquiries in the saloon bar. He was about fifty years old, and sported a loud check jacket which he kept on throughout the interview, despite the heat.

When she had first entered the room he had been quite surprised. Most of his work involved tracking down evidence for divorce proceedings, and he found it hard to imagine any man who was married to this one wasting his time elsewhere.

After he had settled her in a chair, and made a careful note of the name and address, he sat back and said quietly, "How can I be of service to you, Mrs. Newton?"

This was the part Mara had been rehearsing for the past few days. Much as she wanted to know about Patrick Owen, she dare not risk this person uncovering anything illegal. Whatever Jeremy was up to, and she was determined to know that, it was no part of her plan to cause him any trouble.

"I have a half-brother," she confided. "We were always very close, but I must admit he was rather a bad hat in some ways—"

"—was?—"

"Yes. I'm coming to that. Well, the upshot of it all was, there was a big family row, and Patrick agreed to leave the country. People would send him some money from time to time, but he was to stay away, and not communicate with us. Especially with me. My husband was most emphatic about that. Jeremy, that's my husband, is a well-known figure in the City, and he really cannot afford to have his name associated with the kind of scandal Patrick is likely to cause. Is this all clear, so far?"

"Perfectly clear, Mrs. Newton. Please go on. I take it there has been some kind of development?"

Pack of lies, Redman had decided already. Why did they always tell him lies? Look at this one, a face like an angel, and yet she could sit there, trotting out this rubbish about the wicked son who'd been banished to some outpost of Empire. It was the kind of thing that was popularly supposed to happen about a hundred years ago. But not today, Mrs. Newton. Not any more. Lucky the chap was still alive, otherwise she'd have had him bleeding to death in front of a Union Jack, a hundred dead fuzzy-wuzzies in heaps around him.

She was widening her eyes now. Pretty.

"Why yes, there has. How sharp you are."

He made a deprecatory gesture.

"Just experience, madam. Please tell me what's been happening."

"He's back. Patrick is back in England. In London, in fact. Jeremy knows where he is, and he won't tell me. I want you to find out. Please."

Redman pulled at the lobe of his ear.

"H'm. A tall order. This is a very big place, you know. Can you give me any leads, anything I could follow up?"

"Oh yes." Mara was on safe ground now. "Jeremy goes to see him, now and then. The next time it happens I'll telephone you. You can follow Jeremy, get the address, and let me know."

Just like that. Mrs. Newton obviously shared the belief, beloved of fiction writers and the television people, that following a man in a large city was a matter of routine. Still, it was a start.

"Yes," he nodded. "We might have something there. Certainly worth a try, anyway. Let's consider the practicalities."

They had talked for half an hour, during which he explained some of the difficulties for the man who was doing the following. But they arrived at a rough and ready plan of action. Redman tried to make it clear that the plan might be aborted at the first few tries, owing to the density of traffic, the jostling tube crowds, and so forth.

"We'll get there in the end, Mrs. Newton, never fear. The only thing is, I must make it quite clear to you that this kind of venture can be expensive. I'll be as reasonable as I can, but you'll be paying seven pounds an hour in daytime, ten pounds after six p.m. Plus expenses. Taxis, fares, and so on. You'll run up a couple of hundred pounds in no time. It could easily be more."

Mara thought of the sums of money recorded in that desk-drawer of her husband's. A couple of hundred pounds? Small beer.

"It will be worth it," she decided. "Such a long time since I've seen my dear brother. Oh yes. Well worth it."

That had been a fortnight ago. Since then, Jeremy had made two of his expeditions. She had contacted Mr. Redman immediately, and he had been successful in following Jeremy the first time he left the office, but lost him when he suddenly flagged a passing taxi and disappeared into the beehive of Trafalgar Square. By the time Redman had acquired a cab of his own, there were a dozen in front of him from which to choose.

The second occasion had been two days ago. This time they had been lucky, and the red-faced man had been able to follow his quarry right to his destination. Even then, he had had to make some further enquiries before he could be quite certain of his facts.

He was certain now, and wondered what the gorgeous Mrs. Newton was going to say when he made his report.

Here she was now, coming through the door, so he'd soon know.

Mara was radiant today. Ever since Mr. Redman's telephone call, she had been in her happiest mood for many weeks. The great mystery was about to be solved. Let Jeremy go around thinking what a clever sod he was. She would know exactly what was going on. Well, not exactly, perhaps. Not at first. But once she knew where to locate Mr. Gangster Owen she'd be very disappointed with herself if she couldn't find out the rest.

"Well, Mr. Redman, success at last. You have the address, you said."

"Yes, Mrs. Newton, I have it here."

He handed over a slip of paper, written in his square, legible hand.

Mara clutched it triumphantly, and read it. M'm. Good address. It went nicely with that Mercedes of Owen's.

"I am so excited, I can't tell you," she smiled. "Tell me, did you happen to get a glimpse of him? Of Mr. Owen, my brother, that is?"

Redman coughed gently.

"No, I'm afraid not, madam. Tell me, is your brother perhaps married?"

She wrinkled her brow.

"Married? Not to my knowledge. Why do you ask?"

"Because the flat is registered in the name of a lady, you see."

Ah. Well, that wasn't to be wondered at. Patrick Owen would be no stranger to women. How intriguing. Mara wondered what she'd be like.

She shrugged.

"Well, these days that sort of thing doesn't raise eyebrows the way it did ten years ago. What's this lady's name?"

"Tate," he told her. "Mrs. Veronica Tate."

ELEVEN

The meeting between the two men had not been a happy one. When they had embarked on the venture, they had a common goal and an agreed path to follow. Each was content with the contribution made by the other—Jeremy the man behind the scenes, Charlie the man of action. It had worked, what's more, and there was nothing to suggest their success would not continue. In one sense, it was that very success which now brought them to the brink of major disagreement.

A series of developments in their very different private lives had directed each man gradually to a position opposite the other. Charlie wanted to speed things up, Jeremy wanted to slow down.

"A year?" exploded Charlie. "You have got to be out of your tiny mind, my old son. Twelve months? Twelve days'd be more like it."

Jeremy had expected a certain amount of resistance, but to meet such total opposition was more than he had bargained for.

"It's getting risky," he persisted quietly. "We have always agreed never to take any risks. There have been several times when we could have carried out an operation, but I was not satisfied that I could guarantee your safety, and therefore we let them pass. You've always understood that before."

Charlie snorted.

"We wouldn't take any risks. We? Me, you mean. I was always the one who stood to get nicked. You wasn't breaking any laws. Still haven't."

"That was our agreement. I've kept my end of it, and you can't deny that."

"So what's different now? All your information suddenly dried up, has it? You'll have to pull the other one."

Jeremy frowned. For the moment, they were at least talking quietly. He must be very careful not to say anything which would alter that. Charlie Hurst was more of a doer than a talker. In his own interests he would be prepared to do so much talking, and no more. After that he would erupt into some kind of action, whether it was wise or not.

"I've tried to explain that," he replied patiently. "We've gone along very steadily, making marvellous progress. We're both fairly rich men, by most standards. And this is what calls for caution, the very fact that we are now people who matter. People whose actions mean something. We're not the couple of small-time punters we were when we started out. Nobody takes much notice when ten or twenty thousand pounds shuffles across the table. Even thirty or forty. But that's not where we stand, Charlie. Not any more. You and I represent almost a quarter of a million. That is important money. It makes us important people. What we did in the past was more or less out of sight, but we're out in full view now. We can't take any chances."

Charlie listened carefully. This Jeremy had never steered him wrong, and was entitled to be heard. But there was a basic flaw in his argument, in his whole position, that he could not be expected to comprehend. Probably the listener did not understand it himself.

The underlying, fundamental weakness in Newton's whole case was that he represented a view that Charlie didn't want to hear. The decision had been made before Newton ever arrived at the flat. Charlie Hurst had been a guv'nor too long, by right of his fists and boots, to be soft-soaped by some university ponce. Charlie knew what he wanted, what he must have, and that was the fastest possible route to his new existence, and away from his old one. All this talk about risks was a load of codswallop.

"Look," he said, controlling himself, "are you telling me that anything's different, from my end? What I'm saying is, do I stand more chance of getting me collar felt next time I bust into somebody's library? Is that what you're saying?"

He was missing the point, thought Jeremy, close to despair.

"No. I'm not saying that. You know I wouldn't send you out on anything chancy. It's what happens afterwards that I'm concerned about."

"Ah." Charlie pointed a triumphant finger. "Afterwards. After we've swung the deal, you mean, made the money?"

"Well yes, naturally."

"Well yes, naturally," mimicked Hurst nastily. "In other words, old son, you mean you might be having to take a bit of a chance for the first time in your life."

Oh Lord, groaned Newton inwardly. If he thinks I'm running away I'll never persuade him.

"It's not that simple—"

"Balls. It's exactly that simple. You might have to stick your lilywhite neck out, and you're getting the shivers."

Charlie was happier now. This was a familiar situation, one he'd been in many times before. Newton was no longer the equal partner. He was a reluctant accomplice, the one who was afraid of the police, or a punch-up. Oh, Charlie knew how to deal with his sort all right. Done it before.

Jeremy stood up.

"I don't think we're going to get anywhere at the moment. The best thing is for me to leave you to think it over. I've explained it all as best I can. I'm sure that this time tomorrow—"

Charlie rose, and faced him.

"Stuff all that," he interrupted. "You're right about one thing, Jeremy. You've talked enough. Now, you can listen for a change. I want some action out of you. Go and start looking for our next move. And don't be too long about it."

Jeremy was white-faced.

"And if I refuse?"

Hurst shrugged.

"Now don't go being a silly boy," he advised.

The man opposite squared his shoulders.

"I'm not afraid of you, you know."

Charlie dismissed him with a flick of his fingers.

"Nobody said you was afraid. But think about it. Done a bit, have you? Bit of boxing, and that? Bit of rugger, at the university was it? You got the build for it. I can just see you, tearing into them doctors, and that. Nobody said you was afraid. You're just out of your class, that's all. Where I come from, the Marquess of Queensberry is the name of a pub. And that's all it is. Don't make me cross with you, Jeremy. I'll put you away if you do."

And so the lines were drawn.

Jeremy had left, fuming. Fuming, and very worried. Because what he had been trying to explain to Charlie Hurst was no more than the plain truth. It wasn't a question of fear. It was a question of reasoned assessment, and his assessment was that further financial moves at this time would be unwise. He was disappointed with Charlie, and even now was hoping that the man would see reason, in the cold light of day.

If he didn't, then there was a real problem.

Charlie, on the other hand, felt quite pleased with the outcome. What it all boiled down to, in simple terms, was that Jeremy Newton had tried to get a bit uppity, and Charlie had squashed him. All very satisfactory. Mind you, if Newton didn't come up with something—but he would. He would.

He'd better.

Be a bad day for him, otherwise.

Mara had made one firm resolution, after the shock delivered by Mr. Redman.

She was not going to get excited. That would be a disaster.

She would keep calm. It was the only way.

Mind you, when she thought of those two, that cow Veronica and her husband, writhing about in that place in—where was it?—Bayswater, that was it, she could kill somebody. Somebody named Veronica. Or Jeremy. Or both. Yes, that would be better still. Both. She'd have them both stretched out on their famous bed, tied hand and foot, and with their eyes open. Oh yes, the eyes must be open, no doubt about it. Open, so that they could see the sunlight flashing from the razor-blade in her hand. No. Not a razor-blade. A real razor, an old-fashioned cut-throat, like old Uncle Arnold used. One of those. She would advance slowly, a maniac gleam on her face—

"Lady."

"Um?"

"Victoria, lady. We're here. The station, Mrs."

The cab-driver's weary face stared at her through the glass.

"Oh." Mara pulled her thoughts together. "Yes. Thank you. I was miles away. How much is that?"

The driver had already lost interest, and was waving to a group of Arabs, indicating that he was free.

The station was hot and airless. With ten minutes in hand before the train left, Mara wandered to the bookstall to buy a magazine. As she ran her eyes along the periodicals, the cover of a child's comic caught her attention. A square-jawed, hero-type in jungle kit, obviously one of ours, was mowing down scores of evil-faced soldiers, obviously some of theirs. He was holding one of those things they have in the gangster movies—what were they called?—submachine-guns, that was it. Lovely sight. Fancy being able to inflict all that splendid mayhem at one press of a trigger. He was taking it too far, of course, this chap. She only needed two people at the wrong end of the gun. Rat-tat-tat. Wouldn't that be marvellous? She'd be able to hear the bullets scrunching into the bones. They'd have to be naked naturally so that she could see the bullets smacking home. Jeremy and Veronica, naked. They no doubt preferred themselves that way, so let it be.

But it was hopeless, she realised. How did one get hold of such a weapon? You couldn't just walk into a shop and tell the man you'd like a nice submachine-gun, please. There'd be a lot of stuff about licences and things. She remembered Jeremy going on about it once, because of that old service revolver of one of his uncles.

A familiar voice interrupted her thoughts.

"Mara dear. Catching the train?"

Please don't let it be Beth Huntley. She couldn't possibly endure that twittering all the way home. Perhaps Beth was just arriving.

"Hallo, Beth. I was just getting something to read."

Go away, you silly bitch, and leave me alone. I've got a double murder to plan. I can't be doing that with you nattering away.

There was dynamite, of course. You didn't have to

have a licence for dynamite, did you?

"—and so I tried to call you yesterday, but you must have been out."

"Yesterday?"

Beth looked concerned.

"Why yes, dear. You seem a bit far away. Are you all right?"

This wouldn't do, Mara realised. She was stuck with this woman for the next forty minutes, whether she liked it or not.

"Oh yes, really. It's just this heat, makes me a bit drowsy."

"It's a perfect devil, isn't it? That's why I'm so uptight about the pool."

"Pool?"

"The swimming-pool, dear. At the school. They're closing it next week on some pretext or other, as I was just telling you. Are you sure you're all right?"

"Yes, really. Have you talked to some of the other mums?"

"One or two, yes. I'll tell you all about it on the train. We ought to be getting our seats."

And so, it was the very normality of existence, the commonplace exchanges of daily life, which gradually filtered away the red thoughts from Mara's mind. All through the journey she was compelled to express views about the futility of the PTA, the dictatorial attitude of the new assistant head, the prospect of calling a meeting to demand explanations, and all the rest of the details which seemed to be upsetting Beth so urgently. It was all very well for Beth. It wasn't her husband that Veronica Tate had her immaculate teeth into. She had a sudden mental image of what it would look like, Veronica and little Reg Huntley.

"I don't think it's anything to smile about, Mara."

"Sorry, no. Of course it isn't. Something quite different just struck me."

The damned woman even insisted on sharing a taxi from the station.

Free of her at last, Mara arrived back at the empty house. The children wouldn't be home for another hour yet. She wandered about, opening doors and windows to get some air into the place. Something was nagging at the back of her mind, and she couldn't for the life of her identify what it was. Very irritating. It must have been something she'd been thinking about before Beth Huntley appeared. There had been precious little chance of any independent thinking once that lady had launched into her tirade.

What was she doing before that? Let's see, she'd been at the book-stall. The comic, with the death-or-glory merchant in the front. No, it wasn't that. She was opening a window in Jeremy's study when it came back to her.

Uncle Donald's old revolver.

Jeremy kept it on top of a tall bookcase, where the children couldn't reach it, or even see it. Dragging a stool across, she climbed onto it, and reached around. Hard metal brushed her flexing fingers, and she got a grip on the thing and lifted it down. Mara knew next to nothing about guns, but she knew the huge weapon in her hand was almost twice the size of those things the police always had in those crime series. Why, some of those people even tucked them under their arms or down the waistband of their trousers. Not much chance of doing either with this damned great lump. It was all she could do to lift it in one hand. Scrambling down from the stool, she examined the weapon. It had one of those chamber things that went round when you pulled the trigger. Jeremy said Uncle Donald had had it around since the First World War, and strictly speaking they ought to have handed it in to the police years ago. Not that they were doing any harm, and anyway, it would probably become quite valuable in time. These old guns were collected by enthusiasts, and he didn't see why it should wind up being melted down just to satisfy some government whim.

Mara had been examining it curiously when he first brought it home.

"Keep your fingers away from that trigger, dear, whatever you do."

She removed her forefinger hastily from the ring of metal underneath.

"Why? It's not loaded, surely? Not after all these years."

Jeremy knew little more about such things than she did, but men were expected to know about guns, and he wasn't going to admit ignorance.

"Can't be certain," he said mysteriously. "Not with a very old type like that. There could be one up the spout, you see."

She took another look at the weapon, searching for a spout.

"I can't even see a spout," she muttered. "Perhaps it fell off?"

He had laughed at that.

"The spout is the barrel, darling. It means there could be a cartridge, a bullet that is, inside the barrel ready to fire. One would have to muck about with it to find out, and I'm not going to be the one. Lot of accidents caused by people mucking about with fire-arms. Just put it down on the desk, there's a good girl."

The heavy revolver had entered its new life with them in a prominent display position on the wall. Then, when the police had called for the surrender of all unlicensed weapons, Jeremy had decided to put it out of sight. That, coupled with the growth of their normally curious children, had brought the gun to its hiding-place on top of the bookcase.

It was certainly very dirty, she admitted. Bits of fluff all over it, and Lord knew what else inside. But she liked the feel of it, liked the cold anonymity of it. This thing could kill people, she realised, with a thrill. Indeed, it quite possibly had, in the past. What a pity she'd taken no interest in it before, never bothered to question Uncle Donald when he was alive. He was such an old bore at times, with his army stories. She ought to have listened.

Uncertain of her own intentions, she took it into the kitchen, spread a newspaper on the table, and rested the gun on it. At least she could clean the dust off the outside, she couldn't come to much harm doing that. As the blue-black metal began to glow softly under the moving duster, Mara felt an odd affinity with it. They had a secret, these two. She liked the quiet strength of it, the unknown power lying in wait in that unmoving mechanism. The gun was going to be, literally, her hidden weapon. There were half a dozen places she could hide it, where no one would ever look. Only she would know where it was. And then, if the time ever came— No. No. She was not going to start thinking all that nonsense again. She was no less furious with them, of course. Just as hurt, wounded, betrayed. But that frightening redness had gone from behind her eyes. In the first minutes following her discovery she had little doubt that she would have killed the pair of them out of hand. If they had walked into that man Redman's office, and there had been a gun on his desk, she could well have picked it up and fired and fired and fired. That had been an instant, jungle reaction, and she could see that now.

Not that she had any intention of bowing down under the new circumstances. Not by any means. But indiscrimate lashing out was not the answer. There would be no great dramatic scenes, with people striking attitudes all over the place. None of that wronged wife bit, not for Mara Newton. It was such an insulting position to admit to when she thought about it. The kind of thing that happened to dowdy little women, who spent all their time darning children's clothes and on other domestic chores. Not to her, not Mara, an undisputed beauty in her own right. Wouldn't they love it, too, some of those old cows. Love to see her humiliated in the one area where they suspected she would be the undoubted queen. And Veronica, of all people. She'd taken a pretty high tone over Mara's little escapade with the fisherman. Naturally, why shouldn't she? She'd probably needed that Greek holiday to get some rest in that direction. A bit of recuperation. Knowing that when she came back there'd be Jeremy waiting to drag her into bed. Others too, no doubt. Why should a woman like that content herself with just one extra man? She probably had them scattered all over the home counties, the bitch. That was why she had that flat in Bayswater, of course. Couldn't be any other reason. Why had she never mentioned it? Look at that time they'd have to change at Jeremy's office before going to some reception or other. Veronica had known about that, but she didn't offer her flat, did she?

Oh no. That was needed for other purposes. And Mara would soon have a very good idea of her activities. Mr. Redman would be looking into them. It would take a little time, he'd explained, but that was to be understood. Mara was in no hurry now. There was still the unexplained alliance between Jeremy and Patrick Owen. With so much money involved, that had become even more important than before. All these people thought they were so bloody clever, carrying on their plots and intrigues behind her back.

Jeremy, Veronica, Owen. All of them.

Well, before too long, she'd have the whole story. She would know exactly what was going on, in every direction. And when she knew it all, then she would make her move. At that moment she had no preconception of what that move might be, but whatever it was, there was going to be only one undisputed victor at the end. That was going to be Mara Newton.

In the meantime, she would keep cool. Everything must be normal, no changes of attitude, no alterations in the daily round. Just cool.

She took one final rub at the heavy gun on the table.

"No more bookcase for you, old boy. I have a nice warm spot for you, upstairs."

TWELVE

Jeremy Newton looked at his watch. Twenty past ten. Lord, how the evening was dragging. He should never have agreed when Mara had suggested having twenty or so people over for drinks around the pool after dinner. It was probably their turn, he had to admit. They had, after all, been to several like functions in the past couple of months. The unusual summer had brought with it this new idea, of people getting together in the post-dinner period, not for any particular reason, but simply to share the heat. It had proved rather beneficial. Instead of sitting at home, frowsting, and getting bad-tempered, people had to get togged up in something reasonably civilised, and exchange courtesies with their neighbours.

Yes, it probably was their turn, but it was a pity Mara had chosen this particular evening. Still, one good thing was it forced him to think about something else. Something other than the break-in which Charlie Hurst would be carrying out in a few hours' time. Jeremy didn't want it, hadn't wanted it from the beginning, and had made his position quite clear.

Unfortunately, Charlie had also made his point, and forcibly. That had been a stupid thing to do, just when everything was going so beautifully.

"Ah, Jeremy, just the man. Is there any more ice, old boy? This bucket's empty."

"What, already? What are they doing with it? Chucking it in the pool?"

Where the devil was Mara? She ought to be looking after people, not going missing at her own party. It was difficult to know exactly where everyone was at these outdoor affairs. The lighting was scattered, and the moon was only at half-strength. The guests were dotted about in groups, a few actually sitting on the edge of the pool, with their feet in the water. Straining his eyes through the patches of gloom he tried to locate his wife. She ought to be easy enough to spot in that bright yellow thing she was wearing. Well, half-wearing. There wasn't enough of it to describe it as a dress.

Veronica appeared suddenly, with another empty ice-bucket.

"Complaint about the service, darling," she said brightly. "Ah, I see you've already got one of your own. Let us go to the kitchen, there to repair the damage."

Jeremy immediately lowered his voice.

"Do you think that's wise? For us to go inside together?"

Veronica clucked her tongue. He'd never make a conspirator, this one.

"What could be more natural, silly man? I'm not

going to make an assault on your virtue, you know. Too bloody hot, for one thing. In any case, I don't do kitchens. Still, if you're worried. Hey, Tommy. We're heading for the ice-cap. Come and give us a hand."

They trooped off towards the house. Jeremy muttered, "Haven't seen Mara, have you? She seems to have been missing for ages."

"Oh? No, I hadn't noticed. She was making sheep's eyes at Francis when we first came. Fancies himself in the ram department, my Francis. Perhaps they've gone off to discuss next year's lambing."

Jeremy was horrified. The thought of Veronica's husband and his wife—no. That was nonsense. She'd be around somewhere.

"You don't seriously think that? Not in my own house? That would be a terrible thing to do."

Veronica's tinkling laugh echoed against the night.

"What a shocking old hypocrite you are. Think of us, yesterday afternoon. Ah, Tommy darling, good. I was asking Jeremy to hold this ice-bucket between my shoulder-blades as we walked along, but he's taken a high moral tone. It won't worry you, will it, dear? Oh, that's marvellous. Heavenly man."

They wouldn't go for hours yet. There was no point. Nobody could get to sleep until the small hours, anyway.

Charlie Hurst would make his move at two o'clock. Jeremy hoped desperately the plan was going to work. There would be disaster for them both if it didn't. He was quite sure of that.

This was the worst part.

The waiting.

Charlie had spent a boring evening, drinking his heavily diluted scotch and playing cards. Everyone had agreed it was to be no more than a friendly game, with a one-pound limit, so that the lesser fry could join in. For Charlie, who took his cards seriously, this put the evening on the same level as playing Happy Families with a nursery school. Nice for the kids, but not much in it for the grown-ups.

He was glad to make his escape at midnight.

"Not pushing off, are we, Charlie? Not walking out with all the winnings?"

It was only a friendly joke. Charlie had made about twelve pounds in two hours. He'd spend more than that on a round of drinks.

"You know the old saying. He who wins and walks away, lives to win another day."

Irish Tony laughed.

"You got the last line wrong, Charlie. You ought to have said 'drags some poor cow in the hay'. We all know what your game is."

This brought general approval. Charlie Hurst had announced at the outset that he had to leave early. There was a little darling whose husband was on nights, and she got frightened by herself. It was the kind of thing they expected from him, and no one doubted his story. Why should they?

And now he was in the flat at Parkside South, getting ready to leave on his raid. It was his first visit there that day, and he'd been pleased to find a buff envelope on

the mat. Inside it was the official confirmation of the
change of ownership of one Mercedes motor-car. The
new owner was Mr. Patrick Owen, other details
unchanged. It was just one more step on the road to the
disappearance of Charlie Hurst.

He sat staring at the sketch plan for the last time,
ensuring that no detail had escaped. Taking a
cigarette, he reached for the chunky gold lighter, the
only souvenir he'd kept from all his expeditions. It had
come from the home of that oil company bloke, and
Charlie hadn't had the heart to throw it in the river,
along with everything else. It was just the kind of thing
you'd expect a man of means like Patrick Owen to have
about the place.

Right. He'd got it all pat now. You had to hand it to
that Jeremy. When he came up with information, it
was the real thing. Nothing left out, nothing forgotten.
He'd have made a real good crook, that man. Charlie
smiled. What was he thinking of? Jeremy was a real
good crook. A bit nervous about this job, but you got
that with amateurs. When they got nervous, you had to
jump on 'em. The way he'd jumped on Jeremy. And
perhaps there was something in what he'd been saying.
Perhaps, after this one, they ought to slow down for a
bit.

Anyway, time to be off.

It went smoothly, just as they had discussed. The
wall-safe was within inches of where Jeremy had said it
would be. Real old-fashioned idea, this hiding the safe
behind an oil painting. Charlie ran gloved fingers
gently along the side of the frame, heard the soft click as

the catch disengaged, and swung the picture clear on its hinges. The pencil beam torch lit up the steel front of the recessed safe. Charlie reached out.

Suddenly, the room was flooded with light.

"Stand quite still. You're under arrest."

He swung round, ready to fight, then dropped his hands.

There were four police officers between him and the door. Charlie Hurst was not a fool. Escape was impossible, and fighting for the sake of a fight was a mug's game. He couldn't understand how they'd got there.

"Well, well," he said softly. "What's all this, then? Parked on a double yellow line, have I?"

"That's enough of that. Just come along quietly. What's your name?"

"Robin Hood. What's yours?"

He walked towards them, a puzzled man.

The clock above the duty sergeant's desk stood at seven twenty-five when Detective Inspector 'Nobby' Clark reported for duty. He exchanged a series of good-mornings with various officers as he made his way down the corridor to the duty inspector's room.

"Morning, Webbie. Nice quiet night, was it?"

Dick Webb yawned and scratched at his tousled hair.

"You must be joking. Place has been more like a bleeding railway station, all night, instead of a police station." He waved towards the piles of green and yellow forms. "Nice bit of reading for you. Keep your mind off Page Three."

Clark grinned.

"Have you seen this morning's? They couldn't get all of her on one page. Half of her spreads over to Page Four. Any good 'uns in there?"

He pointed to the desk.

"The usual mostly. There's one you'll like though. Got an old mate of yours downstairs. Charlie Hurst."

Clark's smile disappeared instantly.

"Charlie? Well, well, Hasn't murdered somebody, has he? I hope it's King-size Saunders. That would clean the patch up a bit, those two out of the way at one go."

Inspector Webb shook his head.

"If I wasn't so anxious to get at the eggs and bacon, I'd keep you guessing what he was done for. But I'm too tired to play games. Charlie Hurst was caught in the act of burglary."

"Burglary?"

Surprise and disbelief registered in the one word. Webb nodded.

"Red-handed. Had his hand actually on the safe when our people had him."

Nobby Clark whistled softly.

"I don't get it. Where was it, the Bank of England? Can't see Charlie getting mixed up in anything much smaller."

"That's just it. You'll see what I've said in there. There wasn't much more than a couple of hundred quids' worth of stuff a man could shove in his pockets. Private house. Some City bloke. Rich man, and all that, but not much in the way of loose articles."

Clark shook his head.

"Something funny going on. Charlie Hurst? Burglary? It doesn't hang together. Charlie's an important man, not a sneak-thief."

"I know," agreed Webb with a weary shake of his head. "But you can't get away from the facts. Not his first job either, judging by the stuff on him."

"Oh? Could I see that, then?"

"It's on the table."

Dick Webb got up from the desk and walked across the room to a table where a number of large brown envelopes rested. He looked at the labels, picked one out, and opened it.

"There you are. You can see for yourself."

Nobby Clark put a hand inside and took out a miniature camera.

"This is nice," he observed. "Was this from the house?"

"No. He had that in his pocket. Must've nicked it somewhere else. Matter of fact, we might be lucky there."

"Oh?" Clark was interested at once.

"Yes. The photographer last night was Blair. You know, he's a real genned-up man on cameras. Well, according to him, there was a special article about this particular model in the Amateur Photographer a couple of months ago. It's the very newest thing, it seems, lots of special gadgets which they haven't been able to do at that size before."

"So?"

"So, as it's so new, and very expensive, over a thousand pounds, they've only turned out a few to see if there's a market at that price."

Clark nodded, comprehending.

"I'm with you. The importers have kept notes about who they sold them to. So we'll be able to get Charlie for a second burglary, once we've found out who lost this. Won't take long to call on them."

"Right. In fact, we might already know, because if you look in the bag again you'll find that Charlie's been calling on a bloke named Patrick Owen, over at Parkside South. Got the bloke's car registration in his pocket, so perhaps he's nicked the car as well. Anyway, it's a good place to start with the camera before we waste time calling on the other people who bought them."

Clark looked around for the vehicle document, and read it.

"Mr. Owen ought to be very grateful to us. Have you contacted him yet?"

The night-man shook his head.

"No point in dragging him out of bed at three in the morning. I thought you'd probably like to take a ride round there a bit later, Charlie being such an old mate of yours and all."

"You're right there. Yes I'll take Mr. Owen the good news when I've had a chance to read this lot."

Irish Tony was bored. For the past hour he'd been breaking the ends of matches and flicking them indiscriminately around the bar. It amused him to see people jump when something suddenly hit the side of their neck, or when they found wood floating in their drinks. One or two of the victims knew who was responsible, but they weren't looking for a row with Tony. Particularly when they saw that Mad Jimmy Evans was sitting with him. They were wise too, because Evans was building up for one of his eruptions. Nobody knew the signs better than Tony, and he wished Charlie would show up and take charge.

The thought of Charlie made him look at his watch again. Nearly two o'clock. That dolly must have given the guv'nor a good working over last night for him to be this late. Even so, it was time he showed up. It would be chucking-out time soon. Blimey, look at that.

"Hey, Jimmy."

"What?"

"Lamp the poofter at the door. Him in the whistle."

Evans looked sourly over. Tony was right. The new arrival was worth a look. Among all the open-necked shirts, string vests, and even bare uppers, the man in the charcoal lightweight suit looked distinctly out of place. He seemed to be looking for someone in the crowded bar. Then his eyes lit on the two watching men, and he began to make his way towards them.

"He's coming over here," whispered Tony.

"I can smell trouble," muttered Evans.

The man in the suit stood, looking down at them. Then he leaned very close.

"Afternoon, gents. Name is Joe Billings. Got a message for you from Mr. Hurst."

They looked at one another. Evans scowled.

"Who might you be, then?"

"Don't want to talk in here, if you don't mind. Could we get a breath of air? Walls have ears, you know. Old saying."

"What d'you reckon, Jim?"

Jimmy Evans shrugged. It was all one to him. If this geezer had a message from Charlie they'd better hear it. If it was some kind of trick, and there was a team waiting outside for them, well that was all right, too, He'd welcome a bit of exercise of that kind.

"Can't do any harm," he said, non-committally.

Outside, there were a few men standing around drinking their beer. No strangers.

"Got a car over there," pointed the stranger. "Quiet inside."

All three men got into the car.

"Now then, what's the big mystery?" demanded Tony.

"Charlie's been nicked," returned Billings. "He wanted word brought to you."

Nicked? But what for?

"What's he supposed to have done? And where do you come in?" queried Evans.

"Burglary," was the reply. "They've got him dead to rights. He'll have no chance. Mr. Herriott says so. It was him sent me."

Herriott was the high-priced lawyer who looked after their interests. If he was in it, it must be serious indeed.

"I don't get it. Burglary?"

Irish Tony's face was a study. Evans nodded in

agreement.

"You'll have to tell us a lot more."

Billings told them all he had been able to glean. They listened in astonishment, unable to believe the story, but knowing it had to be true. No sane man was going to risk telling a tale of this kind to two such well-known artists as themselves.

"The thing is," Billings concluded, "Charlie reckons he was shopped. They were waiting for him. Mob-handed. And he knows who it was."

"Shopped?"

They both said it at the same time. They were the only people who had anything on Charlie Hurst. Each thought immediately of the other. But the stranger had foreseen that, and said quickly, "Man named Newton. Do you know him?"

This was getting worse.

"No," Tony replied, for both of them. "Who's this Newton?"

Billings explained that Charlie Hurst had not been forthcoming with any details about Newton, or his connection with him. It was a personal matter, he insisted, but he didn't want it left until he got out of the cage. Newton would have to have his bottom smacked.

"Where do we find him?"

Jeremy Newton sat in the garden, an untasted drink by his hand. Today had been one of the longest of his life. Jeremy had grown up to a code, and what he had done had broken that code at a crucial spot. He had betrayed a comrade, and he'd known better than that since he was four years old. Oh, the circumstances had left him no choice, Charlie himself had left him with no choice. In the end, his action would be vindicated. Charlie would serve a few months, no more. In that time, attention to Jeremy's City movements would have lessened considerably, because he intended to do absolutely nothing. People would assume he had been like so many, a promising new comet, which turned out to be no more than a shooting star. He had made a lot of money, but no more than plenty of others. When it came to the final push, the big gamble which would make him a financial power or a pauper, his nerve had failed him.

That would be the judgement and he was content to leave it that way. Later, when Charlie had served his sentence, and had a month or two away on holiday, they would strike again, bigger than ever.

Nothing was changed, really. They could have done it his way, the only sensible way, and yesterday need never have happened. It was Charlie who was really to blame, not him.

But Charlie was sitting in a prison cell, and he was sitting in the dark comfort on his own garden, staring at the stars, a free man.

Was that a car turning in? It sounded like one, but there were no further sounds. Must have been a trick of the wind. At least he didn't have to try making conversation with Mara. She had given up an hour earlier and gone to bed.

Two men appeared suddenly on the patio in front of him. Nasty-looking types. Strangers.

"What the hell are you doing here?" he demanded, leaping to his feet. "Who are you? What do you want?"

"Now, now, don't get all worked up," advised one. "It is Mr. Newton, is it? Mr. Jeremy Newton?"

"Yes, but—"

"That's all right then," said the other. "We've got a message for you. From a friend."

He smacked one hand against the other. Moonlight reflected against metal. Good God. Were those knuckledusters? The french windows were open, ten yards away, and behind Jeremy. If he could get to the telephone— They took a step towards him. Grasping the heavy chair in his right hand, he swung it in a great arc in front of him, hitting one man hard and catching the other a glancing blow.

They both cursed and stumbled. He was off now, racing inside the doors and pulling them quickly shut, shooting the bolt. Snapping on the lights, he grapped up the telephone. There was a crash as a boot came through the glass doors. Then another. A hand reached inside, feeling for the bolt. Jeremy snatched up a heavy ebony ruler and smacked at the hand. There was a yowl of pain, and the fingers withdrew.

"Hallo, hallo," he was shouting into the telephone.

Upstairs, Mara was unable to sleep, and sitting beside the bed, fanning herself, when she heard the crash. What the devil was going on down there? It sounded as though Jeremy had had a drop too much and fallen through a window. Well, she couldn't leave him to bleed to death.

There was a roar of pain now. But that was not Jeremy's voice. Moving quickly to the window, she stared down.

The two men had stepped back a yard from the shattered doors.

"After three, we go in," announced one. "Ready? One. Two. Three."

They charged forward together, and there was a splintering of wood and glass.

She could hear Jeremy shouting into the telephone. "Hallo, hallo."

They were going to kill him, Mara decided. There wasn't time to think about why. She had to do something.

"No use shouting into that, Jeremy old son," advised Irish Tony. "We cut the wires, see?"

"Didn't want to be disturbed like," added Evans. "You made me cut my shoulder, Jeremy. That's gonna cost you extra."

They waded into him. Jeremy managed to get in a few blows, but he had only his fists, and he was out of condition. His attackers used metal rings over their knuckles, and their boots into the bargain. Jeremy went down, striking his head painfully against the desk as he went.

They began to kick him, methodically and with well-aimed boots.

"Get away from him, or I'll shoot."

The woman's voice from the doorway took them both by surprise.

Mara stood there, clad only in a flimsy piece of pink netting, with Uncle Donald's old revolver held out in front of her in both hands.

Irish Tony whistled.

"Well, look at this. Looks as if we're going to have some afters, Jim."

Evans nodded.

"You'd better put that thing down, missus. It hasn't been fired since the Crimean War."

Mara was nonplussed. Neither of them seemed remotely afraid of the revolver. She didn't know quite what to do next.

"Jeremy. Can you get up, Jeremy?" she shouted.

But Jeremy was no more than a crumpled heap on the ground.

"Old Jeremy's sleeping it off, love. Why don't you and me go and try a bit of the same?" grinned Tony, taking a pace forward.

"Take one more step and I'll fire," she screamed.

"Don't be daft, love, that thing should be in a museum."

Tony walked confidently towards her.

"I warned you."

Mara yanked at the trigger with all her strength.

There was a blinding explosion from the gun in her hand. For a moment the tableau froze.

Mad Jimmy Evans said hoarsely, "Oh, Christ. Oh, Christ."

The two men watched helplessly as Mara sank to her knees, blood gushing noisily from the jagged hole in her throat, where a chunk of metal from the exploding revolver had lodged.

Neither man moved as they heard the police car pulling up outside.